I'm Not for Sale

GINGER RODEGHERO

Published by Richter Publishing LLC

www.richterpublishing.com

Book Cover Design: Richter Publishing image from 123rf

Editors: Margarita Martinez & Kate Sabol

Book Formatting: Monica San Nicolas

ISBN-13: 978-1-945812-80-4 (Paperback)

DISCLAIMER

This book is designed to provide information on sex trafficking only. This information is provided and sold with the knowledge that the publisher and author do not offer any legal or medical advice. In the case of a need for any such expertise consult with the appropriate professional. This book does not contain all information available on the subject. This book has not been created to be specific to any individual people or organization's situation or needs. Reasonable efforts have been made to make this book as accurate as possible. However, there may be typographical and or content errors. Therefore, this book should serve only as a general guide. This book contains information that might be dated or erroneous and is intended only to educate and entertain. The author and publisher shall have no liability or responsibility to any person or entity regarding any loss or damage incurred, or alleged to have incurred, directly or indirectly, by the information contained in this book or as a result of anyone acting or failing to act upon the information in this book. You hereby agree never to sue and to hold the author and publisher harmless from any and all claims arising out of the information contained in this book. You hereby agree to be bound by this disclaimer, covenant not to sue and release. You may return this book within the guaranteed time period for a full refund. In the interest of full disclosure, this book may contain affiliate links that might pay the author or publisher a commission upon any purchase from the company. While the author and publisher take no responsibility for any virus or technical issues that could be caused by such links, the business practices of these companies and/or the performance of any product or service, the author or publisher have used the product or service and make a recommendation in good faith based on that experience. All characters are fictitious. Any resemblance to other real persons, living or dead, is purely coincidental. The opinions and stories in this book are the views of the authors and not those of the publisher.

DEDICATION

To the survivors of human trafficking
May your souls find peace.

CONTENTS

ACKNOWLEDGMENTS

Thank you to Richter Publishing for working with me to polish my thoughts, it resulted in a much improved story for you to enjoy.

INTRODUCTION

I wrote this book to raise the awareness that human trafficking (slavery) still exists in our society today and to show how easily one could possibly be caught in the trap. The work is fictional but I have personally met and assisted individuals that were trafficked and needed a helping hand to return to normal life.

CHAPTER 1

The low light in the bar cast distorted shadows on the walls as the packed room of women twisted and snaked to the harmonious beat. Sydney's long black hair was draped over her deep-set, dark eyes. Tucking a stray strand behind her ear, she tried to focus on the face in front of her. The mouth was moving but the words were muddled among the jumble of sounds. Sydney felt like a fog was overtaking her and then ... nothingness.

Shelby bolted upright, her sheets soaked and tremors wracking her body. Was that a dream? Where was Sydney? It was so real! Crawling out from her warm cocoon, Shelby tried to clear the remnants of the nightmare. Reaching out mentally to find Sydney, she realized the connection she had shared with her twin sister since ... well, before she could even remember, was gone. How could that be? Sydney had always been there. But now, body shaking, Shelby felt as if she were stranded in a desert, with no connection to her only lifeline.

The dim light in the dorm room at Assumption College outlined her roommate's small frame huddled under a pile of blankets. Pacing the room, trying to calm her nerves, Shelby struggled to put the pieces together. Nothing made sense. The only thing she knew was that Sydney wasn't in her head anymore.

Thinking back, Shelby recalled her first connection with her identical twin. They must have been only three, climbing among the boxes in the small storage room at the back of their parents' Albanian market, where they were left to their own devices more often than not. She could still hear her father's rebuttal to their mother's concerns—"What trouble can they possibly get into?"—followed by his husky chuckle.

Straddling the boxes of Turkish coffee, olive oil, and Raki, Shelby had slipped and become wedged between the crates of rough wooden planks. The more she wiggled, the further she slid into the box cave.

Then she heard it. "It's okay. I'm here. I'll help you."

Shelby, choking on her tears, saw dark eyes peeking between the crevice. It was like peering into a mirror. No words were spoken, but Shelby knew her sister was there. As Sydney pulled her from the small cavern,

Shelby felt a flow of energy seep through her sister's small hand into her body. She was wrapped in a warm radiance that soothed every nerve of her tiny frame.

She really needed to feel that link right now. It had been the one stable part of her life and had pulled her through so many difficult times. Now, staring out Nault Hall's third-floor window, Shelby felt as blank as the desolate street below.

Snapping out of the memory, she grabbed her phone from its charging dock. *Is Sydney all right? What was that dream all about?* Horrible images raced through her mind as she stabbed the number two, speed dialing her sister.

Come on, come on. The phone rang over and over, eventually rolling to voice mail.

"Hi, this is Sydney. Leave a message and I'll get right back to you." Shelby dropped the phone on her bed.

Sydney was a freshman at Wellesley College, an hour and a half from Assumption, where Shelby was majoring in global studies. This was the first time they'd ever been apart in their life. Right now, the strain of the distance was unbearable.

Sydney's good at these things, Shelby thought. Her twin always had the solution to any situation. Shaking her head, Shelby was blank. How could two people who looked so alike be so different? Before they'd left for college they'd had identical yin and yang symbols tattooed on their wrists. Since getting the tat she had gotten into the habit of gently rubbing the design. It served as a forever reminder of their personality differences: Sydney the eternal optimist, Shelby the pessimist.

Slivers of moonbeams peeping through the blinds outlined the clutter on her desk. The matching twin beds and armoires filled the space, but something was missing. She didn't feel like the dorm room was really hers; it was missing the homey feel, it was missing...... What was it missing? As a tear rolled down her cheek she realized, it was missing Sydney.

Her roommate stirred. Holding her breath, she stood motionless until Brittany settled back into a peaceful slumber. *No need to disturb her,* she thought. *I'll wait until morning.* Shelby crawled back under the mountain of covers. Closing her eyes and wishing for sleep, she only felt the void of Sydney's absence.

######################

Shelby, jarred by the creaking floorboards as her roommate snuck across the room, sat up, still feeling the emptiness of her sister hanging over her head like a storm cloud.

"Sorry, I was trying not to wake you." Concern edged into Brittany's voice. "I heard you up last night.

Everything okay?" Brittany stood in front of her dresser brushing her blonde waves into a tight ponytail. She eyed Shelby, waiting for a response.

"Yeah," came a blunt response. Throwing back her covers, Shelby dashed toward the bathroom, not wanting to get into the conversation. She needed to figure out what had happened to Sydney.

Standing under a hot stream of water, she replayed the vision from the night before over and over in her mind. The dream had to have something to do with the fact that she had lost Sydney's connection. The only logical conclusion was that something horrible had happened to her twin.

What do I do? I've got to get to Wellesley, but how? An answer popped into her head like a weasel popping out of a hole. *David!* He had a car; he'd do anything for her. He'd been chasing after her since they met on the first day of class … kinda annoying. Really, the last thing she wanted was to encourage his attentive behavior. Searching her mind, Shelby found no other option. She hadn't made many friends in the six weeks she'd been at Assumption, preferring to keep to herself. Her solitude was backfiring on her.

Stepping from the shower into the steamy room, she wrapped a terrycloth robe tightly around her slight frame. Clearing a small circle in the foggy mirror, tears pooled in her dark eyes as she stared at her sister's face

5

looking back at hers. Her black, wavy hair accented the sharp features they shared.

Jerking open the bathroom door, she was relieved to see Brittany sitting on her bed, tugging at her fur-lined boots.

"Do you have David's number?"

"Really? Now?" Brittany was clearly shocked. She'd been encouraging Shelby to go out with David for weeks. Shelby felt confusion radiating from her roommate as she grabbed her phone from the backpack lying on the floor.

It was a quick phone call. David sounded shocked to hear her voice. Shelby gave him a quick excuse about her sister having a problem last night and needing her help. He didn't even hesitate when she explained she needed a ride to Wellesley. He'd said he'd be there in a few!

######################

Forty minutes later, Shelby was sitting in the passenger seat of David's 2000 red Accent staring out the window, watching the scenery flash by, not taking note of anything in particular. Shelby was locked in a trance. She'd been unable to shake the feeling that something horrific had happened to her sister. The nightmare plagued her mind.

David had promised no questions, but she could feel his brown eyes boring through her, as if he were trying to read her thoughts. Curiosity finally won.

"So where are you from?" His voice cracked as he broke the silence with a harmless question. Try as he might, it was obvious that David wasn't great at this "getting to know a girl" thing.

"I grew up in Worcester. My parents have a store there."

"What kind of store?" She felt a bit sorry for him as he struggled to make polite conversation. *Maybe the drive will go by faster if I participate.*

"They've had an Albanian market since before my sister and I were born. They immigrated from Kosovo before things got crazy over there." She watched him closely to see if she could detect any adverse reaction. Growing up she'd experienced varying levels of disapproval and harassment when she mentioned her nationality. Kids could be so harsh.

David's reaction caught her off guard. "My grandparents live in Worcester. Maybe they've been to that store. They're from Albania." He paused. "I'm a second- generation American."

"I wouldn't have guessed. You don't have … well, you look so American." She rolled her eyes as the words came out. That sounded so stupid. Sydney was so much

7

better at small talk. She would've had David's whole life story out of him by now.

"My mom is actually of Native American descent, so I guess I'm part of the great melting pot. But I know a bit about Albania. I love my grandma's cooking." He was beginning to sound more relaxed as the miles ticked by.

"Yep, Albanian food is the best. I think that's why my parents kept the store, so Mom would have an endless supply of the things she loves to cook." The tremors that had been racking her body were ebbing now that her mind was distracted. David gave her a quick smile and for the first time she realized he was a sweet guy.

"So, I don't really know the history of what happened in Kosovo?" He sounded genuinely interested. Shelby jumped in quickly, telling the part of the story she was all too familiar with.

"Well, what I know comes from my parents. They had just been married in '98 when things started to flare up between the Serbs and the Kosovo Liberation Army. My parents, being young, decided it was a sign to start their life elsewhere. My grandma's sister sponsored them to come to the US. She'd been here since the fifties and owned the store my parents took over. A year later, my sister and I were born. Actually, that was on the day the genocide started. I guess we were really lucky to be here in the States." She saw David nodding as if he really understood.

"My grandparents came here in the fifties too. I wonder if they knew your grandma."

"Grandma's sister, my great aunt," Shelby gently corrected him, feeling a spark of enthusiasm. She had surprised herself by going on as much as she had, but this was a topic she loved to talk about and the reason she had enrolled in Assumption's global studies program.

"So, you and your sister are twins?" David caught her off guard by switching the topic. Scowling, Shelby turned back to the window, the small ember of interest quickly fizzling. David had crossed a line.

Catching the hint, he retreated. "Sorry," he mumbled, drumming the steering wheel.

He does deserve some explanation, she thought. *After all, I got him out of bed and he agreed to help, not even knowing what he was getting into.*

"Yeah, we're identical. Usually, only our parents can tell us apart." This was a topic she hadn't discussed since they were eight. One day she'd told their teacher that she and Sydney had special powers. They'd never heard the end of it that whole school year. Kids! Then there was the "incident" that had happened in high school. She'd felt like such a freak. Shelby shook her head, trying to purge the remnants of the past.

"I just know she's in trouble. I really appreciate you bringing me to Wellesley." She crawled back into her shell and returned to watching the tree-lined landscape roll by.

Feeling her distance, David sank deeper in his seat, focusing his attention on the long stretch of the Massachusetts Turnpike. The black ribbon of highway, lined with conifers and majestic oaks, gave one a feeling of a tunnel leading to an uncertain destiny.

CHAPTER 2

Shelby woke to a gentle nudge of her shoulder. "Oh sorry, I didn't sleep much last night." Righting herself and straightening her hair, she felt a flush rising in her cheeks. She hadn't meant to nod off, but the scenery rolling by had put her in a trance. Trying to orient herself, Shelby realized they were on Main Street of the quiet college town. She watched students rushing toward their futures.

"Hey, no problem. We're just getting to Wellesley. I'm not sure where you planned to go." David's voice cracked, negating his efforts to sound natural.

Jeez, thought Shelby. *Plan? What plan?* She shrugged noncommittally. "I guess I really didn't think that part out. Sydney always took care of the plans."

"How about we get some coffee, a campus map, and figure it out?" David's suggestion calmed the emotions that were beginning to percolate.

"Yeah, coffee. I do better with coffee."

"How about the Peet's over there?" He swung his Hyundai into a vacant spot, hopped out, and raced around the car to get the door. Stepping from the car, Shelby rolled her eyes. She wasn't used to this kind of attention.

Pulling open the glass door to Peet's, a wave of coffee aroma greeted Shelby. Inhaling deeply, she could almost feel the caffeine race through her blood. The place was full of students getting their morning fix. She noticed two girls with their heads together sitting at the mahogany counter. Surveying the pastries under the glass dome, her stomach rumbled.

"Hungry?" David broke her concentration.

"I suppose."

"Get what you want, it's on me." David was being way too generous.

"You can't. I've already imposed too much. I can't let you." She didn't want to get over her head with this guy, no need to lead him on.

As she stepped to the counter, she was greeted by a way-too-chipper student. *No one can have that much energy at this hour,* she thought.

"I'll have a caffé mocha and an everything bagel with strawberry cream cheese." Shelby whipped out her debit card, shoving it at the smiling face. She couldn't help but notice David shrink back, stuffing his hands into his jeans. Stepping aside, she waited for her order while David paid for his coffee … black, no sugar. He picked up a campus map sitting next to the register.

Following her to a vacant table in a far corner, he spread the map across the table, smoothing out the wrinkles as if he were ironing a crumpled shirt.

"Sydney!" The voice came from across the store. Shelby's eyes searched the room to see if maybe her sister was there. That was when she saw the two girls from the counter headed her direction.

"So, Sydney, who's this? What will Karl say?" A tall blonde dressed in black leggings and a navy Wellesley hoodie gave Shelby a suggestive nod.

"I'm not Sydney."

Then, as if the sun had just risen, the girls' faces lit up. "You must be her twin! Sydney mentioned she had an identical twin. WOW, you look exactly like her. You even have the same tat." The blonde didn't even pause to take a breath. Words flowed from her like sap from a tree.

Shelby shrugged. *I've been hearing those words my whole life, she thought, except for the part about the tattoo.* She wished she could melt into the wall. Shrinking her hands into the sleeves of her jacket, Shelby realized she had been stroking the tattoo as if she were rubbing a crystal ball. Could it reboot her connection to her sister? *I gotta find Sydney!*

Reaching deep, she summoned a shred of courage. "Have you seen Sydney this morning? I'm here to surprise her."

"What about last night?" David interjected. Shelby kicked him under the table. She saw the shock on his face, but it served its purpose as he slumped back into his chair and clammed up.

The blonde jumped back in. "We haven't seen her since she went off to some 'hot' party" She made air quotes around the comment. "I really don't think she's been very nice lately. If you want to make friends, you have to be a friend. It's just that ..." she rambled on before Shelby interrupted.

"Um, what about a party?" Shelby remembered her dream. Sydney had been someplace where there was lots of loud music.

"Don't know, we weren't invited," sarcasm dripped off the blonde's tongue. "I think her roommate invited her. They've been really buddy-buddy lately. It's kinda weird if you ask me. Like I said, she's just not being very friendly."

I didn't ask you, thought Shelby, but instead of voicing her thoughts she forced a quick smile.

"Wow, even your smile is exactly the same. How's it feel having a carbon copy of yourself?" The blonde didn't quit.

Her friend grabbed the elbow of her hoodie. "Let's go. We need to get to class. Nice to meet you." She nodded as they darted toward the front door.

Shelby exhaled loudly, watching them walk away. That was a perfect example of why she kept to herself.

"Well, we know something," David interrupted her thoughts. "She went to a party with her roommate. How about we go find the roommate? What dorm?" He scratched his chin, studying the campus map.

"She's in Shafer House. Should be easy to find … looks kinda like a castle." Shelby took off outside while David struggled to refold the map.

Standing in the warm sun, Shelby could feel the effects of her morning jolt. David headed for his car.

"Go on, I can walk." Shelby was already feeling indebted and didn't need an additional obligation added to her current concern.

"No, it's all right, I don't have class today. I can hang out and give you a ride back after you find your sister."

Shelby shrugged and headed toward David's car. "Campus is that way." She pointed toward the sprawling stone buildings nestled among the conifers. It was a picturesque view, like one you would see on a postcard. But looking toward their destination, a chill shot through her body that even the morning sun couldn't melt. Shelby was certain something horrible had happened to Sydney.

######################

As soon as David pulled into the campus, Shelby recognized where she was. She'd been here twice before with Sydney—once when Sydney first looked at the school and then the day she helped her sister move in. Sydney had a turret room on the third floor of Shafer Hall. She'd been so excited to have the view.

Hopping up the three steps to the entrance, the dorm's heavy wooden door swung open as a student raced past, throwing a backpack over her shoulder. Shelby grabbed the handle and inched in with David following close behind. Shelby recognized the sounds of young women going about their morning routine.

Walking through the common space she was greeted by several girls calling her Sydney. She didn't bother to explain. Hopping into the elevator at the end of the hall she punched the number three and waited while the doors slowly shut out the world. As they groaned closed, she heard someone yell, "Hey, Sydney! Wait!"

Too late. Saves the explanation anyway, she thought.

Stepping from the elevator and heading down the hall with David lagging behind, she felt a prickly sensation over her entire body. Was that Sydney or just nerves?

"Hey, how are you going to get in the room? You don't have her key, right?" David, trying to be helpful, stated the obvious.

"I'll knock." Which was exactly what she did when she stopped in front of 327. The door slowly opened and a petite, dark-haired girl peered through the crack.

"Sydney?"

Shelby wasn't sure if the expression she saw was one of shock, surprise, or confusion.

"I'm Shelby." If only she had a dime for every time she had said that.

"OH! Okay." There was pure sweetness in the voice. "I'm Christine, Sydney's roommate."

Peering into the room, Shelby immediately recognized which side of the space belonged to her sister. Everything was in order. Pictures of their family adorned her shelves, her college books were neatly stacked on the desk next to her computer, and the blue paisley comforter on her bed was so smooth you'd think it had never been used. Yep, that was Sydney!

"Sorry, Sydney's not here." Leaning against the door, Christine refrained from inviting them in.

Shelby looked her up and down, from her dark messy bun to her sloppy Wellesley tee, blue leggings, and bare feet. Her gaze trailed back up and peered into Christine's dark eyes.

"I was told she went to a party with you."

"Yep, we took the commuter rail into Boston and went to a few hangouts, then we got split up. We were supposed to meet up at the commuter at 11:30, the last train back. But she didn't show. I thought maybe she'd come back earlier but she wasn't here when I returned. She never showed up. Really, I'm kinda concerned." Christine's eyes jumped from Shelby to David and back again, boring through Shelby.

"Who's he? Guys aren't supposed to be up here," Christine snapped. Shelby immediately felt she had violated some sacred code.

"He's with me. I really need to find Sydney, it's important." Glancing at David, she could tell he'd been intimidated by this wisp of a girl. "David, how about waiting in the car? I'll be down shortly." She didn't need to tell him twice. He took off toward the elevator.

"How can I help?" As if a switch had been thrown, Christine was all sweetness and light again.

"This is so odd. Can I just go through her things?" Shelby didn't know what she'd be looking for but she needed to start somewhere and this Christine didn't really seem to have a clue.

"I guess. You're her twin … right?" Christine stepped aside and Shelby walked across the room to the desk she knew belonged to her sister. Rifling through her notebooks, she found a class schedule and Sydney's student pass with her meal plan. *At least I can eat,* she thought, cramming them both into her hoodie pouch. "I guess she had her phone?" Shelby knew the phone wasn't working but she was fishing for clues.

"I think so. I did try to call her last night when I was waiting for the commuter train, but …" Christine shrugged her shoulders like she was completely out of answers.

"Well, thanks." Shelby needed to get out of there and decide what to do next. "Sorry to bother you this morning."

"Oh, no, no, no, it's fine ... She's probably sitting in class right now. I know she has a 9:00 on Friday." Christine ushered Shelby out the door. "Maybe I'll see you later."

"You're right, she's probably in class right now." Shelby heard the lock click behind her. *There's not a chance Sydney's in class,* she thought. *I would just know. I would be connected to her.* She headed for the elevator.

Plopping back into David's car, she pulled out Sydney's schedule.

"Wow, that was intense," David interrupted her concentration.

"Yeah, there was something odd about the whole thing, don't you think?" Shelby was thinking back over the assorted expressions that had played across Christine's face.

"She was intimidating to say the least. Did you get any answers from her?"

"She acted like she had no idea, so it was just very weird." Shelby paused as she tried to figure out the way to Sydney's first class.

"What's next?" David interrupted her concentration.

"I have her schedule. Let's check her first class, just in case. Let's go ..." Shelby jumped from David's car, heading toward the north campus even though she was positive her sister wouldn't be there.

CHAPTER 3

Heading across the quad to Sydney's 9 a.m. class, Shelby was greeted by a dozen or more girls who mistook her for her twin.

"Wow, your sister is really popular," David commented.

"Yeah, tell me about it. I've lived my life in her shadow."

Stepping into Pendleton Hall, Shelby stopped to study the collage painted on the entry glass. "Immigration is Beautiful," it stated. *I'd have to agree with that,* she thought. *If not for immigration, who knows what kind of life my sister and I would've had.*

She headed down the hall to Sydney's class: "News and Politics: Reading Between the Lines." Shelby was all too aware of her sister's passion for political science. Sydney had selected Wellesley because of their Peace and Justice Studies program. She planned to change the world.

She stopped as she pulled open the door to the spacious class, David still trailing behind her. "You better wait here. This is an all-girls school, you know."

"I couldn't help but notice," he commented, eyeing two Asian women entering the class.

"Why don't you wait outside? I won't be long." Shelby ducked into the room, not waiting for his reply. Sliding into a seat along the back wall, she scanned the room hoping to see her twin sitting among the gaggle of girls chatting and settling into their desks. Her heart skipped a beat when she realized that Sydney wasn't in the room. *I knew better than to put hope into this,* she thought as the professor entered the room.

Shelby had planned to slip out of the class once she confirmed her sister wasn't there, but her interest was piqued by the topic on the white board: "President Trump and Twitter." She routinely followed his tweets and was interested to hear the class' viewpoints. Their parents had always encouraged the twins to look at all sides of any issue and then decide for themselves. *Nothing wrong with listening to this discussion,* she thought. *Everyone thinks I'm Sydney anyway. Besides it would be rude to get up and leave.*

Fifty minutes later she was headed back across campus to the dorms. Tapping on the window of David's car, she woke him from what was definitely an uncomfortable slouch.

"She wasn't there." She felt no need to explain any further.

"Where to now?" David stepped from the car, rubbing the back of his neck trying to work out the kinks.

"Coming out of class, some girl said Karl was looking for me … meaning Sydney. I might still have his number. Sydney and I hung out with him some in high school." She was scrolling through her contacts, looking for the next link to her sister.

"Who's Karl?"

"This guy we went to school with. He's been chasing Sydney since freshman year. I think he goes to Olin, studying engineering." She was deeply engrossed in her search as she explained. "Here it is!" She stabbed at the phone like she was trying to reach through to grab Karl. He picked up on the second ring. "Yeah."

"Karl, this is …" before she finished, he shouted into the phone.

"Sydney, is that you? I've been so worried!"

"This is Shelby." She was well prepared for his next comment.

"Wow, I forgot how much you sound like Sydney. Where is your sister? Why are you calling? Where are you? I'm worried about her." He finally stopped for a breath.

Shelby ignored the first comment and all of his questions. "I need to talk to you," she blurted out. Then she realized he might be the only link to her sister. "I'm here at Wellesley, looking for Sydney. I heard you're looking for her too."

"I knew it, I knew it, I knew it … something has happened to her." Distress oozed through the phone.

"Karl, stop!" she yelled. "Where are you?"

"I'm here," he stammered. "I mean, I'm at Wellesley too."

"I figured!" She was annoyed with his hysteria. *I need someone in control,* she thought. "Where on campus are you?" She spoke slowly, trying to mask her frustration.

"Oh." He stopped for a moment, and Shelby imagined him looking around, getting his bearings.

"I'm outside Sydney's dorm. I was hoping she'd come back here between classes. I didn't know how else to find her." His voice choked.

"Look, do you know where Peet's is downtown?" It was the only place she knew and her body was begging for more caffeine.

"Yes, okay. I'll see you there in five." He hung up abruptly.

She looked at David. "More coffee?" He opened the car door as if it were her chariot in waiting. *I can't handle this drama,* she thought. *Two guys who have too much testosterone flowing ... really!*

#######################

Stepping back into Peet's, she immediately recognized Karl huddled at a table in the far corner. He hadn't changed much since she'd last seen him, just a little more rugged-looking with his unshaven chin and unruly blond locks. He jumped up and embraced her like they were long-lost friends. Shelby ducked out of his grasp and plopped into the closest chair.

"This is David." She watched as the two guys sized each other up. Karl's six-foot build towered over David's medium stature.

"He drove me over from Assumption," she added, trying to break the ice between the two.

"Oh." Karl's attention shifted. Shelby saw his wheels turning as he settled in the seat across from her.

"So, you came too? You know there's something wrong? I just knew it when I didn't hear back from her."

He really needs to settle down if I'm going to get anything useful out of him, she thought. She needed to take control of the situation but her social graces were a bit lacking; that was Sydney's specialty. Inhaling deeply, hoping to settle her nerves, she grabbed Karl's hands that were clutched together in the center of the table.

"Yes, Karl, I feel something is wrong." The panic on his face rose to code orange.

"I knew it. I knew it ..." He hung his head, covering his face with his large hands.

"Karl, settle down!" Her frustration jumped an octave. He looked her straight in the eyes, a tear rolling down his cheek.

"It's just I remember all that stuff in high school about you two, you know the whole psychic thing. If anyone would know what happened to Sydney, you would. You being here just proves something is terribly wrong."

Shelby ignored his comments about high school. I just need information, she thought. "Karl, tell me what you know."

"David, get us some coffee, please." She studied Karl as David moseyed to the counter. The fear she felt was reflected in Karl's face.

"You really care about her, don't you?" She'd always figured his traipsing after Shelby was just some kind of puppy love.

"More than you know ... More than she knows."

David returned with three coffees and placed one in front of each of them. Karl reached for his cup, hands trembling. Taking a slow sip, he set the cup down and let out a long sigh.

"I knew she was going to Boston last night," he began. "She was going with her roommate, Christine." He ran his fingers over the stubble on his chin. "I don't know, they've been hanging out lately, but it's weird ..." he stopped. Reflecting on what he had said, Shelby sensed he was trying to sort out some kind of puzzle.

"What's weird?"

Karl was studying his fists as if there might be an answer hidden inside of them like a fortune inside a cookie.

Karl snapped out of his thoughts. "I don't know," he said, shaking his head. "Anyway, I didn't want her to go and I told her so. It's just ... have you heard about the girls disappearing? Three girls have gone missing from

Wellesley and they all disappeared in Boston. Sydney said I was foolish. Wouldn't listen to me. I should've stopped her." Wiping the tears from his face with his sleeve, he added, "It's all my fault. I should have stopped her. I won't forgive myself if something has happened to her."

"Look, Karl, I need you to get a grip. Do you know exactly where she went?"

"No," he replied. "I only knew she was going with Christine."

David, who had been intently watching the conversation, chipped in his two cents. "Looks like we need to go back to the dorm."

"We?" Shelby couldn't contain her irritation. "David, thanks for bringing me here, but you need to head back to school."

"How are you going to get around? I want to—"

Shelby interrupted before he could finish his argument. "I'll be fine. Karl will help ... right?" The grimace on her face told them there would be no further conversation. She grabbed her coffee and headed for the door. David and Karl sat staring at each other like two little boys who'd been reprimanded by their mother.

######################

Using her sister's name, Shelby managed to get a key to the room by explaining she'd forgotten hers when she went to class. She was sitting at Sydney's desk, surfing the web for information on the missing girls, when Christine returned.

She stopped short when she saw Shelby sitting at the desk, the intensity on her face turning to a quick smile. "Did you find her in class?" Sugary syrup dripped from the question.

"No, but I spoke with Karl. He seems to think something horrible has happened to Sydney and you were the last person she was with." Her eyes bored into Christine.

"Oh, that Karl guy. I don't know what Sydney sees in him. You know he's always just hanging around, really annoying. Sydney is too nice to him. I think she encourages his behavior. It's kind of misleading, don't you think?" Christine perched on the side of her bed, dropping her book bag to the floor.

"Yeah, I guess." Somehow in one statement Christine had managed to raise doubts in Shelby's mind about two people she had known for years. "I guess," she repeated, struggling to process what she'd just heard. She'd been ready to interrogate Christine, but now she had lost her whole train of thought.

"So, what are you doing?" Christine peered over Shelby's shoulder, looking at the web search. Shelby

"So, where did you go with Sydney last night?"

"Well you know, we both get along so well, we have so much in common." Christine dodged the question. Pulling books from her bag, she threw them on her bed carelessly.

"Like what?" Shelby was perplexed. Trying to recall any conversation she'd had with Sydney regarding her roommate, she came up blank.

"Well, I'm Albanian and from Kosovo … like your family, we're refugees. It was such a coincidence that we were put together as roommates."

Shelby was immediately sucked in, wanting more information. "Were you born in the US?" She was thinking about her family's history of immigration.

"Oh no, I was born in Kosovo. I was only two when the fighting broke out. My family was finally able to come here a year ago." She paused, reflecting on some distant past. "Those were tough times."

Shelby was well aware of the history of strife in Kosovo between the Serbs and Albanians. It had been a regular conversation when they were growing up as they had relatives stuck deep in the turmoil during the years of unrest.

"I can't image how different my life would have been if my parents hadn't come here when they did." Shelby was actually starting to feel empathy for this girl she barely knew.

"I'm lucky to be here. As a refugee I was able to get financial aid to come to Wellesley. I have an opportunity to gain some knowledge and hopefully go back to help the people in my country." Tears pooled in her eyes.

Shelby was beginning to understand why Sydney would get along with this girl. They shared the same passion.

Christine shuffled through the books on her desk and pulled out a small pile. Stuffing them into her backpack, she headed for the door.

"Gotta get to my next class. If you're here later, I can tell you more. Sydney and I loved talking about our country."

She was out the door before Shelby could say anything. Shaking her head, she realized she'd never gotten an answer to her question. Where had Christine taken Sydney?

CHAPTER 4

Darting out of her dorm room, Christine didn't waste a moment dialing her mom.

"I might have a problem," she muttered as she dodged girls coming and going from Schafer. "Her twin showed up and is asking me lots of questions."

"Twins? Well, that's an interesting development." The soothing voice melted the stress from Christine's shoulders. *Mom has the knack,* she thought. In an instant she was in a dark, damp basement, clinging to her mother's worn jacket. Outside the ruins of the building there were shouts, people running, guns going off, the sound of a helicopter hovering somewhere in the distance. Her mom stroked her matted hair and reassured her they were safe. Christine remembered feeling like her heart would jump out of her chest.

"Christine … Christine, are you there?" Her mother's voice broke in. "Stay the course. I'll speak to your father. Maybe we could use this situation to our advantage."

"But Mom, I'm just freaking out a bit here. Are we safe here in the US or will we be found? I'm always afraid we'll be found." Panic was overtaking her.

"Christine, stop! You're not in Kosovo anymore, you're in the US. It's different. Come on, you're stronger than this. Your father has everything under control. Like I said, just stay the course, play your part." Her mother's voice was firm and comforting at the same time.

"Okay, I've gotta get to class." Christine shook the final remnants of the memory from her brain.

"Don't knock yourself out. You probably won't finish the quarter." Her mom chuckled. "For now, keep your head in the game. You're great at it."

Hanging up, Christine didn't realize she'd been holding her breath as her chest deflated like a worn-out balloon. Her mom had protected her through the harshest of nightmares. Living in America was a cakewalk compared to her childhood in Kosovo.

Okay, I got this, she thought as she surveyed the campus. She'd miss this beautiful setting once they moved on—the giant conifers, the stately buildings surrounding the tranquil lake. As a child she had only dreamed of living in such a peaceful home. *Yep, I'm going to miss this place,* she thought, shifting her backpack and gazing toward the sports center. *So much for class. Right now I think a good workout will clear my mind.*

######################

Shelby stretched her cramped muscles. The day had vanished into dusk while she sat hunched over her sister's desk, searching online. After the conversation with Christine, she'd begun to wonder about life in modern-day Kosovo. Trolling the internet, she'd found an array of pictures, some showing modern cities much like those in the US. Others depicted scenes of war-torn areas that had never been rebuilt and lots of trash. Low wages and unemployment seemed to be a huge problem. Shelby easily understood why Christine's family would want to move to the US. Her search hadn't eased her concerns about Sydney, but it had occupied the afternoon.

Her vibrating phone brought her back to the real world. *Maybe ...* she thought, digging into her hip pocket. Damn. Just Karl. Reconsidering, she retrieved the phone from where she'd just tossed it on Sydney's bed.

"Yeah ... did you hear from her?" She didn't bother to offer any kind of greeting.

"No, I was hoping you had. What are you going to do?" Karl was clearly still in panic mode.

She didn't know where to turn at this point. Checking the time, she realized her stomach was begging for attention.

"Get some food," she replied, searching her pockets for Sydney's meal pass. Digging up the campus map David had acquired, she surveyed the options.

"How about some sushi?" She surprised herself by inviting Karl for food, but for once she didn't want to be alone.

"Meet you in five." Karl hung up without another word.

That's the second time he's done that today, she thought as she stared at the blank screen.

A brisk walk later, she stepped into Bae Pao Lu and searched the small clusters of girls for Karl. She spotted him at the counter analyzing the day's specials scratched out on the chalkboard hanging above the counter.

"The spaghetti squash looks amazing," she said to no one in particular.

Startled, Karl whipped around, finding Shelby studying the board. "Man, that was so like Sydney. I just keep hoping she's gonna turn up like nothing ever happened."

"Well, she hasn't, and I need some fuel to cope." Shelby felt the strain wearing on her.

Minutes later they carried plates piled high with an assortment of California rolls, tiger rolls, tuna rolls, and a side of spaghetti squash covered in pesto and pine nuts.

Juggling the dishes, trying to making their way through the maze of tables, they were greeted by more than one table of girls.

"Hey, Karl!"

"Good to see you two."

"Hey, what's happening, you two?"

They didn't bother to stop and explain.

Nestling into a secluded booth, they spread out the feast so they could both partake of the varied options.

"Water?" Karl suggested, heading toward the beverage kiosk.

"How about some green tea?" Shelby didn't bother to look up as she dug into the sushi. She rolled her eyes heavenward, biting into a California roll dripping with soy sauce. Karl returned and slid the drinks across the table. The only sound between them for a while was the shuffling of plates as they downed the smorgasbord.

"That was incredible," Shelby grabbed her napkin. Wiping the last drops of sauce from her lips, she pushed her plate to the end of the table. "I haven't eaten since this morning. Didn't realize I was so hungry."

"Yeah, I haven't thought of much except Sydney all day." Karl's voice was still strained. "I'm sure you hate it, but I gotta say you are more like Sydney than I ever realized."

"Really. Like I haven't heard that before." Shelby's tone exuded exasperation.

"No, I don't mean in looks. I meant more like … I don't know." He searched for the right words. "Intensity, I guess."

"How's that?" Shelby studied his face.

"I feel like you have the same drive, like you know exactly where you're headed."

"Sydney wouldn't have sat in her room all day on the internet if I was missing. I have no idea where to look." Shelby bit her lip. Despair was settling in as she realized she had no answers.

"What does your gut tell you?" There was a hint of bravado in his voice.

Stroking the tattoo on her wrist, she took a moment to mentally review what was nagging at her. Inhaling deeply, she outlined her thoughts. "Well, I know I can't connect with her. That's only happened once before, in high school, and something horrible HAD happened."

"And ..." She felt as if Karl was trying to pull a mystery out of her.

"I don't know," she paused, not really ready to voice what was on her mind.

"I know you know something. What is it?" Karl wasn't letting her off the hook. He needed answers too.

"Well, I don't really know Christine. It's so strange I don't know anything about her from Sydney. We share everything." She stopped short. *I hope he doesn't ask me what Sydney has shared about him.*

"What about Christine?" He didn't miss a beat.

Dodged that bullet, she thought.

"Well, she puts me in a spin. One moment I get one flow from her, the next minute I get a different feeling. I can't read her. She's ... distracting." Saying those words helped her to clarify some of her afternoon's search. She hadn't really wasted her time. She needed to know how this girl operated, and there was something in the information she had gathered that would fit the pieces together. She just had to find it.

"That's it. Sydney does the same thing—she studies people and really understands their behavior. Just when you think she's only being social, she comes up with something profound about a person's behavior. She's very intuitive. You are too!" Karl looked deep into her eyes, like he was reading a crystal ball.

"I don't know, Sydney's always been centerstage. I just follow her lead. I've always felt when the cell split, all the positive stuff went to her. I need her to make me whole. That's why I have to find her." A tear dropped on her tattoo. She rubbed it firmly, as if it would produce some mystical insight. "Besides, she would do it for me."

"Hey, Sydney," a sassy voice interrupted her thoughts. "Karl isn't giving you a hard time, is he?"

Looking up, she saw it was the tall blonde from Peet's. Shelby rolled her eyes, not wanting to get into a conversation with her.

Karl to the rescue. "This is Shelby." The force in his voice stopped her cold.

"Ohh," was all the blonde said as she retreated.

"Thanks." Shelby offered a strained smile. "I can't deal with girls like that."

"That's what I mean, neither can Sydney."

"But they all still like her anyway." The comment was punctuated with her signature shrug.

"Look, what do you think we should do next?"

"We?" she asked sharply. Shelby paused when she saw the hurt on his face. She lightened her tone. "Okay, in the morning if I haven't heard from her, I'm going to go to the police. You're welcome to come, but you don't have to."

"Yes, I do! We're in this together." This time his tone made it clear there was no discussion to be had.

"All right, you're coming. Now I need to get some sleep. Last night was rough." She gathered the plates and headed to the nearest bin.

"I'll walk you back. I can't have you disappearing too."

On their walk back, Shelby decided it was time to confront her mom. Sending a quick text, she kept it vague. *I'm at Wellesley visiting. We'll call in AM. Shel.*

An answer shot back. *Great, dear, you two have fun. L, Mom.*

"Shouldn't you tell her more?" Karl's concern was fair.

"I'll wait till tomorrow. Maybe Sydney will show up. No need to worry Mom." Shelby knew it was an excuse, but she was too tired to deal with it.

CHAPTER 5

Trying to slip quietly into her sister's dorm, she couldn't help but feel like she was breaking in. Really it wasn't her room, but she needed a place to stay tonight. Christine, pounding away on her keyboard, started when the door creaked open.

"I thought maybe you went back to Assumption."

"How did you know it was me?" No one except their mom could tell them apart in an instant. Besides, Shelby shouldn't have had a key.

"Just figured." A no-answer. Christine acted as if it was the most natural thing in the world. "I was hoping you would come back. I thought we could get to know each other. You know, since we're both from Kosovo."

That was the last thing Shelby wanted to do, but she needed to find Sydney and this girl was the last person to know her whereabouts. Mustering up some courage, she offered a slight smile.

"Yeah, let's do that. Let me find something comfy first." Digging through Sydney's dresser she pulled out polka-dot lounge pants and a matching T-shirt. Slipping into the fleecy bottoms and "Will Wake for Waffles" tee, she grabbed a pillow from Sydney's bed and snuggled into the lounge chair situated between the beds. Christine's eyes tracked her every move.

"What are you working on?" Shelby struggled to break the ice.

"Oh, just doing some research. Do you have any news about Sydney?" Christine swiveled around in her chair and pulled up her sleek, dark hair.

"It seems no one has seen her. Karl and I are going to go to the police in the morning." Shelby watched closely to see if her comment produced any reaction, but Christine was completely distracted with her long locks, arranging them in a neat bun.

"It seems you were the last person to see her." Shelby was determined to get whatever information she could extract from this girl.

"Well, not really. I left her with a group of guys at some party," Christine responded nonchalantly, wrapping her arms around her knees.

"Where was the party? Who were the guys?" Shelby's impatience seeped through.

"You know, it's all a blur to me. We were hopping from bar to bar and I don't really remember which one we were at when I last spoke with her. I feel so bad." She hung her head. "I wish I could be more exact. I can't imagine how worried you are." A tear rolled down her cheek.

Shelby backed off, feeling a hint of guilt. "I didn't mean to upset you. I just need to find my sister."

"I've lost so many people in my life. It just brings back so many sad memories." Grabbing a tissue from the box on her desk, she dabbed at her eyes.

"Oh I see. I can't imagine what life was like for you growing up." Shelby remembered the strain in her own home as a child. Every day there had been conversations about this aunt or that cousin who were stuck deep in the Kosovo conflict or had been displaced in neighboring countries. At the time she didn't really understand her parents' anguish, but looking at Christine now, she recalled their torment.

"So how old were you when the war broke out?" Shelby asked softly.

"I was only two, but I remember being dragged from place to place. It was like a giant hide- and-seek game, and I was always afraid to be found," she paused. Shelby could see that Christine was running pictures of her past through her mind.

"It's all just bits and pieces. I think my mom tried to stay calm for me but I could always feel her panic. My dad was part of the KLA."

"Really?" Shelby interrupted, shocked. She knew a bit of the group's history from her earlier web search.

"The Kosovo Liberation Army was a group of Albanians who formed an army to fight against the Serbian suppression. The Serbians would kill the KLA's family members if they could find them. I remember sitting in dark hideouts, cuddled against my mom, her heart hammering." Christine stopped short, deep in thought. "Afraid to be found," she muttered.

"Did your father survive?" Shelby whispered.

Christine snapped out of her trance. "Oh yes ... when the war ended he joined the Kosovo police force, but then we had the opportunity to come to the US." She stopped and gave Shelby a smile. "Things were rough, but we're here now and safe."

The story tugged at Shelby's emotions. "I'm glad your family is safe. I know so many lives were uprooted or lost. Sounds like you were the lucky ones."

"If you can call living through a war lucky, I suppose." Christine got up and ambled across the room. Digging through her drawer, she came up with a small travel bag. "You know, I had a spin workout earlier. I think it's time for a shower." Throwing a towel across her shoulder, she left the room without another word.

Shelby sat quietly, going over the conversation. She remembered the endless discussions her parents had when she was young, but she had never talked to someone who'd actually been there, trying to survive. She realized, as a child, that the war wasn't real to her. The war had been real to Christine. Shelby tried to imagine the impact it would leave on a person.

Her thoughts were interrupted by her phone. Grabbing it from Sydney's desk, she saw David's name. *Hmmm, do I really want to deal with him right now ...* Taking a deep breath, she accepted his call.

"Hi, David." Closing her eyes, she tried to rub the exhaustion from them.

"Hey, Shelby, I was calling for an update. I hope you don't mind." David paused, waiting for an answer. "Shelby?"

"Yeah, David, I'm here." Strolling across the room she looked out into the quad. Students were darting on their way to who knew where. Shafts of sunlight dappled through the conifers as the sun slipped into the west. Where had the day gone?

"I assume you're still at Wellesley? Do you know anything yet?"

"Nothing." She didn't mean to be short with him but she had no desire to give a rundown of how little she'd gotten done since he'd left.

"What are you going to do?"

"If I don't hear anything from her by morning, I'm going to the police. Karl's coming."

"Karl?" Envy seeped through the phone. "You know I would help in any way."

Jeez, I don't have time to juggle the insecurities, she thought. "Look, David, I'm gonna go there in the morning; if there's something you can do to help, I'll let you know. But for now, concentrate on school." She couldn't ignore David's heavy sigh. *That sounded a bit cruel,* she thought. *I wish I could be more sensitive like Sydney.*

"What about your classes?" David labored to keep their conversation alive.

"I'll go online and check for notes." Even as she said it she knew she was too exhausted to even care. "I promise I'll call as soon as I know anything." She forced compassion into her voice.

After a long pause, David answered, "All right, talk to you then."

"Yeah," she muttered as she hung up.

Crashing into the pillows on Sydney's bed, she stared at the blank ceiling, searching for the lost connection to her sister.

#######################

In the dark of the night, Shelby awoke in her sister's bed. Trying to adjust her eyes to the pitch-black, she felt like she was floating in a fog. Sitting up and finally fully awake, she felt Sydney reaching out to her. She could see the vague outline of a cramped space. Where was Sydney? One thing Shelby knew for sure was that her sister was distraught. Usually their communication was so clear; she struggled to sort through the haze that was flooding her mind.

As Shelby tried to pull the pieces together, she sensed her sister's fear. Her own body started to shake violently. Never had something like this ever happened between them. Never had her sister not had control over a situation. Even that time in high school, she had been able to pull the strands that linked her to Sydney and find her twin.

This time was different. Sydney was being restrained in some way. The space was dark and seemed ... well, was it a concrete bunker? *Where is she* ... struggling, Shelby tried to make sense of the images coming through. She knew Sydney's life depended on it.

Suddenly Shelby felt a warm rush through every cell of her body and then, in a flash, the connection was gone.

"Nooooo!"

Christine bolted up out of her bed. "What, what, what ..." The rude awakening had left her in a dazed confusion.

"Oh crap, I'm so sorry I woke you up." Shelby was huddled in the corner of her sister's bed, trying to calm the tremors that were wracking her body.

Christine switched on the small light next to her bed. "What happened? You look like you saw a ghost!" She crawled into the bed next to Shelby and gently wrapped an arm around her shoulders. "You're shaking. Are you cold? Can I help you?"

"No, I'll be okay." Shelby shrugged off Christine's arm. "Really, it's okay."

Christine headed back to her side of the room and crawled under her down comforter. Reaching up to switch off her light she glanced over at Shelby still huddled on her sister's bed. "Are you sure?" There was genuine concern in her voice.

"Yeah, I'll be fine." Shelby lay back on the pillow and took a deep breath, trying to calm her racing heart. *I'll be fine ... but I don't know if Sydney will be*, she thought as she closed her eyes.

CHAPTER 6

Shelby got up before the sun and snuck out of Sydney's dorm, trying to avoid Christine. Bundled in her sister's Wellesley hoodie she headed across campus for her wake-up jolt at Peet's. It was a brisk walk. Fall was knocking on summer's back door.

Stepping into Peet's she did a quick once-over, making sure to avoid the small table of girls who she'd seen yesterday in Sydney's class. After picking up her order, she made for an empty table in the back corner, circumventing random students who might mistake her for Sydney. The coffee surging through her system warmed her chilled bones. Taking a nibble from a chocolate croissant, she relished the brief pleasure.

Finishing the last bite, she wiped the crumbs from the table in front of her, then pulled out her phone and searched for Karl's name. She wondered if he'd stayed at Wellesley last night or if he was an hour away at Olin, sleeping in his own comfy bed. She didn't want any delays in putting her plan in action. He picked up on the second ring.

"Shelby?" He sounded like he was waiting for her call. "Where are you?"

"I'm at Peet's!" He hung up before she could ask his whereabouts. *He has got to stop doing that,* she thought.

Before she finished her coffee, she saw Karl jerk open the front door and do the same once- over of the coffee shop that she had done only minutes before. Spotting her, he scurried through the maze of tables, and in what seemed a nanosecond, was standing in front of her. The same panicked look from yesterday was still plastered on his face.

"Wow, is your name Flash? Were you waiting around the corner or something?" She was a little perturbed that he had hung up on her. He cringed at the irritation in her voice as he settled in a seat.

"I've been up for a while, waiting on your call. I didn't want to wake you. I was headed this way when you called. I needed to …" As he rambled from one thought to the next, Shelby could tell he was still freaking out.

Reaching across the table, she squeezed his hand, stopping him mid-sentence. "Hey, it's okay. Get some coffee and we'll go over my plan." She tried to sound composed. *Someone has to keep their head together,* she thought.

"Okay, good idea." He jumped up and headed for the counter. He took two steps and turned back. "Can I get you another?"

"Thanks, that would be great!"

Shelby didn't waste any time searching her phone for transportation to Boston. She decided the best option would be to take the commuter rail right outside Peet's. She could use her sister's ID. Karl had his own. Glancing at the time, she realized they needed to get moving if they were going to catch the next train. She gathered her belongings and headed for the door, meeting Karl halfway.

"What's up?" Holding two coffees and a bag of who knows what, he turned to follow her.

"Just come on, we gotta hurry." The perplexed look on his face stopped her briefly. "Well, are you coming or not?" She didn't wait for his answer as she bolted toward the door.

#######################

They caught the 8:46 to Back Bay. After showing the conductor their IDs, they headed for a seat in the back of the nearly empty car. Few students were heading to Boston early on a Saturday morning. Shelby settled into a seat next to a window. Karl slid in alongside her. She grabbed the coffee he was still juggling and took a big gulp. Closing her eyes, she settled her head against the back of the seat and tried to calm her nerves. Replaying the visions from the night before over in her mind, she began to shake.

"Are you okay?" Karl asked, placing his hand on her arm. "What's happening?"

Shelby normally would not share her and her twin's "connection" with others, but she knew Karl's concern and felt safe letting him briefly into her world. Explaining the visions, she saw disbelief on his face.

"What is that like? Being so connected?" There was no ridicule in his voice, only curiosity.

"I truly don't know how to explain it. It's been there my whole life. It's part of who we are." She saw that he was trying to understand the unique relationship. "I really don't know what it would be like to not have her ..." Shelby stopped. "No, I know what it's like now. It's almost like a part of me has been cut out." A tear rolled down her cheek.

Karl grabbed a tissue from his pocket and quietly offered it to her. Lost for words, he settled back as the rails clicked on and the landscape reeled by. They rode the rest of the thirty minutes in silence.

When the train pulled into the terminal, they gathered their bags. Within minutes they were on the curb, trying to figure out the way to the Bay Back police station. Karl pulled up a search on his phone and found the station was a few short blocks away. From the number of people coming and going through the door they could tell the place was already abuzz.

Stepping into the station, they were rapidly engulfed in a wave of people. The sound was deafening, but despite the confusion it seemed everyone else knew exactly where they were headed.

"Who do we see?" Karl had no idea what to do next.

Shelby felt like a leaf being blown in the wind, bumping from person to person, working her way through the throngs of people. *Sydney would know exactly what to do,* she thought.

"Okay, let's stop and figure this out." She grabbed Karl's sleeve and pulled him against the wall. Scanning the room, she noticed a glass-enclosed counter with a lady officer pointing directions to an elderly man who tipped his hat and moved off in the direction she had indicated.

"Over there." She headed toward the counter with Karl in tow. Standing in front of the closed glass window, she waited nervously for the lady officer behind it. When she finished shuffling papers, she slid the pane aside.

"Can I help you?" Her stern face was pulled into a grimace by the tightly wrapped black bun nestled at the base of her neck.

Shelby took a deep breath. "Excuse me, please …" she glanced quickly at the officer's name badge and started again. "Excuse me, Officer Randel. Where do I report a missing person?"

"How long has the person been missing?" Officer Randel was all business.

"For a day, I guess." Shelby was caught off guard by the officer's demeanor.

"The person needs to be missing for forty-eight hours before we can file a report."

Shelby was shocked, not expecting that response. She couldn't imagine what might happen to her sister in forty-eight hours! She was about to open her mouth and give the officer a piece of her mind when Karl interrupted.

"Thank you, Officer Randel. Who do we report to when forty-eight hours has passed?"

"The missing persons division is on the second floor. They'll complete a full report and turn it over for investigation." Officer Randel stopped for a moment and looked into Shelby's eyes that were pooled with tears. "It's okay, honey. Whoever is missing is probably just sleeping off a weekend party." Her manner softened slightly. "This is the college party district, so we see this all the time. That's why the forty-eight-hour wait. You'll see." She slid the window closed with a flick of her hand and snatched up a ringing phone.

Shelby felt a rage boiling inside her. Karl noted her expression and steered her toward the door. Once outside, Shelby cut loose.

"Can you believe that lady? She didn't ask one question about who was missing, what she looks like, or why we think she's missing. What does she mean she sees this all the time? This isn't like any other time! I just know something terrible has happened." When her rant was spent, she crumpled into tears.

Wrapping his arm around her shoulder, Karl scanned the streets for a place to regroup. Leading Shelby across the street, he made a beeline for Starbucks.

####################

Karl deposited Shelby in a quiet corner and made for the counter to retrieve the magic elixir. When he returned, he found Shelby completely lost in thought, gently rubbing the yin-yang tat on her wrist.

"Is that like rubbing a crystal ball?" He set a steaming latte in front of her.

"What?" Shelby started from her thoughts. "What were you saying?"

Karl shrugged. "Just saying, does rubbing that thing help your connection?"

Shelby glanced at her wrist. She'd been totally oblivious to what she was doing. "I wish. It doesn't work like that," she muttered.

"I know, just trying to lighten the moment." He trailed off when he saw the expression on her face. Sliding into the seat opposite her, he realized for the first time since the whole ordeal began that Shelby seemed shattered.

"So, what do you plan to do next?" He quietly broached the subject.

She stared into her coffee and shook her head in defeat. "I was counting on the police to do something. I'm not good at this. Sydney is the one who figures things out. She just always seems to know what to do." She returned to staring into her coffee as if some solution would spring from the bottom of the cup like a jack-in-the-box.

"I don't know …" Karl stumbled in his thoughts, "You seem to be figuring it out pretty well so far." He needed her to keep it together. She had the connection that could find Sydney. "Listen, since we're here, why don't we visit some of the spots she might have been to and see if anyone remembers seeing her or talking to her?"

"That might work," she glanced at her phone, "but it's a bit too early for them to be open."

"We have all day. What do you want to do in the meantime?"

Karl watched her face as she studied the coffee, hoping she would snap out of it. She took one last sip and then looked him straight in the eye.

"Tell me about these other missing girls. Did you know them? Has anything been found out about their disappearance?" Her wheels were turning.

"I really don't know anything, it's just all over the local news to be careful and stay in groups. Sydney thought I was being paranoid."

Shelby grabbed her computer from her bag, logged into Starbucks' Wi-Fi, and started a Google search. She typed in "missing college students in Boston" and started trolling the results.

"What are you thinking?" Karl studied the intensity on her face. She had gone from defeat to action as if a switch had been thrown.

"I know something horrible has happened to her, but maybe she's not the only one. I need to find out what happened to the other girls. Maybe they're all connected." Scrolling through the search results she found an article that sent a frigid chill to her very soul.

"What?" Karl was stunned by the shock on her face.

"It says here that the three cases have been turned over to Detective Lt. Down of the state police."

"What does that mean? Who's she?" Karl was starting to freak out all over again.

Shelby stopped and studied his panicked expression. "She runs the state Human Trafficking Unit."

"What does that mean?" The tension in his voice jumped a decibel.

"It means my worst nightmare could be true." Shelby's eyes filled with tears.

CHAPTER 7

"Has anyone located Kovac yet? He took my money and I want it back!"

Five men were huddled around a rough wooden table. Cigarette fog formed a thick haze in the dark, dank room. No one ventured an answer. They'd all experienced the vengeance of Vladimir before.

"He's been gone nine months and no one has gotten a lead on where he took off to?" His dark eyes flicked from one man to the next, his most trusted followers. They were letting him down. He didn't like it.

"He took off in the night with his wife and kid. They just vanished. You know how clever he is," Luan ventured an excuse.

"We've been over that; I don't want to listen to your sniveling. I want results." Vladimir's rage was coming to a boil. Losing Jetmir Kovac had put a major dent in profits. They all knew that Jetmir managed the girls and profits better than Vladimir. They also knew that Jetmir was tired of playing second fiddle.

Jetmir and Vladimir had grown up together in the small town of Zubin. They'd been the first from their village to join the rebel KLA when Serbian forces began the ethnic cleansing of Kosovo. Jetmir and Vladimir had fought side by side as thousands of homes were destroyed and hundreds of thousands of Kosovars were displaced or killed. When the war ended, some of the KLA joined the National Liberation Army, but Jetmir and Vladimir had hooked up with the Kosovo Protection Corp. They'd quickly climbed the ladder of authority and in no time found themselves in the senior positions of organized crime.

Pacing the cramped room, Vladimir rubbed his gnarled hands over a stubbled chin. He stopped short. "He's got a wife and kid. It should be easy to track them down. Maybe he changed their names," he paused, "maybe he's set up shop elsewhere. Get creative … FIND HIM!"

Fortunately for Jetmir and his family, no one had thought to look outside of the European Union … yet.

#######################

Shelby and Karl cruised the net gathering info. Lt. Down headed the state Human Trafficking Unit and worked closely with the Department of Children and Families. DCF's job was to investigate any reports of human trafficking.

"I wonder why these cases were turned over to Lt. Down." Shelby searched the articles, looking for any clue that linked the stories.

"No idea. They just warn girls to stay in groups and in busy places. It's all hush-hush about them." Shelby felt the strain in Karl's voice.

"It says here her passion for this line of work is because she once rescued a fourteen-year-old prostitute. I can't imagine being forced into that kind of life at any age, much less fourteen. Listen to this: 'The depth of their victimization and the amount of control these men had over them was impossible to forget.'" Shelby quoted the article.

"Do you think that Sydney is ..." Karl choked on his tears.

"I don't know. I just know something is wrong and I need someone who can help me find her." She stopped a moment to give Karl a chance to collect himself. "Hey, you know what, let's go see if we can find anyone who saw her. Where did you guys hang out most?" she asked gently.

Karl inhaled deeply, trying to pull himself together. "Well you know how she likes to dance. There's a couple of places we'd go if she was in the mood. Mostly we would hang out at the Whitehorse. But who knows where she might have gone with Christine."

"Yeah, well let's just start at the Whitehorse and see if anyone saw her." Shelby jumped up, stuffed her computer in her bag, and looked at Karl expectantly. "Let's go. Which way?"

Karl followed her through the maze of tables and chairs out to the sidewalk. He looked both ways, getting his bearings. "This way."

#######################

It took a moment for their eyes to adjust as they stepped into the dim light of the Whitehorse. It was late morning ; two guys were knocking balls around on a pool table, otherwise there was no activity. The barkeeper nodded to them, then continued shuffling glasses from one rack to another, preparing for the evening onslaught.

"What next?" Karl asked as he surveyed the unusually quiet surroundings.

"Let's just find out if he saw Sydney on Thursday." Shelby made a beeline for the man behind the bar.

Sliding onto a wooden stool she took a moment to get her thoughts together. Sydney would have jumped right in and been best friends with this guy in minutes.

"Hmm, excuse me." It came out so muddled she wasn't sure if he'd heard her.

"Yes." His baritone voice and sky-blue eyes caught her by surprise. She was instantly tongue-tied. "Can I help you?" There was genuine sincerity in his tone.

Flustered, she felt a flush race across her face. "I'm sorry to bother you," she stammered.

"It's no bother, I'm not busy now," his eyes darted around the room. "Waiting for the lunch crowd, but it's usually late afternoon on Saturdays before we start to pick up. What would you like?"

"Nothing. No, I mean I don't need any food or drinks ..." her train of thought had completely left the station.

Karl, seeing how rattled she was, stepped in. "We just had a couple questions for you about a ..." he paused, not knowing quite how to put it.

"I've seen you two in here before." He directed the comment to Karl.

"Yes, well, no ... me, yes, but ..." Karl stuttered, trying to explain everything at once.

Shelby had finally gained control of her thoughts and jumped in, saving Karl from further embarrassment, "You've seen him in here with my twin sister. That's who we wanted to ask you about."

"Wow! You look exactly like—"

"Yeah, yeah. Listen …" she glanced at his name tag, "Steve." She drilled his baby blues with an intense stare. "I need to know if you saw my sister in here on Thursday night. She's missing and I just want to know if you saw her with anyone in particular."

"Jeez, Thursday was two nights ago. After a while they all run together. This place is usually packed and I don't really keep tabs on who comes and goes," he rambled, looking off into an invisible nowhere as if he was surveying a file of pictures. "Yeah, I did see your sister in here. I'm not sure if it was Thursday, but she was with that foreign girl."

"That's it," Shelby jumped in, "she was out with her friend on Thursday. Did they stay long? Did they leave together? Were they with anyone else?"

"Hold on, hold on," Steve put up his hand, halting the barrage of questions. "I did see her, yes, but beyond that … you've got to understand, I'm really busy here at night. I'm not here to babysit the students."

Shelby shrank away from his irritation. "I understand, I'm just so worried," a tear rolled down her cheek. "I'm just trying to find someone who might have seen her."

"Have you been to the police?" Steve's tone returned to its normal mellow timbre.

"Yes, but we can't file any kind of report until she's been missing for forty-eight hours. I can't wait that long ... I just know something is wrong." The urgency in her voice caught his attention.

"How are you so sure something is wrong? Kids do stupid things. They go home with someone else, forget to call, then show up like nothing ever happened."

Now he's sounding like the police officer, she thought.

"Not Sydney! Look, I just know!" Shelby glanced at Karl. No way was she going into a long explanation about her connection with her sister.

"Sorry, that's all I know. She was here with that dark-haired foreign girl. Can't tell you when she left or who she left with." His tone made it clear he was washing his hands of the situation.

"Okay." Shelby noted that Karl was clearly as disappointed as she was. "Where to next?" Karl shrugged.

They headed toward the door; Steve went back to stacking the glasses. "Wait," he called. "The foreign girl ...the girl with the accent..."

"Yeah, what about her?" Shelby got a shiver down her spine, anticipating his response.

"I've noticed her before. It's hard not to, if you know what I mean. I've noticed that she's always in here with a different girl, every time. Only one girl, always a different girl, only one time. Next time, different girl. I always thought it was strange because you know how girls hang together." He smiled at Shelby as if there was a secret sisterhood that he was somehow privy to.

"Yeah," Shelby agreed, even though she had no idea what he was talking about.

"Anyway," he shook his head as if he was trying to make sense of the oddity. "I haven't had time to give it much thought, just noticed it."

"Thanks." Shelby walked away.

"Hope it helps." Steve waved his bar towel.

"Maybe." Shelby grabbed Karl by the coat sleeve and darted out the door.

"What's up?"

"I don't know. His comments about Christine ... something about it gives me the creeps. Is it possible that the other girls he's seen her with are the other missing students?"

"Whoa, whoa, whoa … you are jumping to a crazy conclusion." Karl backed away as if to avoid getting mixed up in that idea.

"Am I?" She drilled him with an intense stare.

"Shelby, now you're freaking me out." He shuddered as the implication hit home.

"Come on, we're going to some of your other hangouts. I have some new questions I want answers to." Shelby took off with renewed intent.

"Wait, hold up. Do you know where you're going?"

She stopped short. "No, but you're going to lead the way! Let's go."

By the time they had hit three more pubs, Shelby had no more information than she had gathered from Steve. Yes, some had seen her sister; no they didn't really notice who she was with; no, they had no idea who she left with. The barkeeps all seemed to be oblivious to what was going on in their establishments. Someone could vanish right in front of their eyes and they would go right on serving up drinks and food to the next person in line.

Sitting on the bench at the bus stop, Shelby was exhausted from the lack of sleep and endless worry. She had put so much hope into returning to the scene of the crime and now she was walking away in more confusion than before they came to Boston.

"What are you thinking?" Karl interrupted her silence.

"First I'm going to get some rest," she looked at his exhausted face, "and you should too! I'll figure it out in the morning. Look, this is our bus."

Climbing aboard, they settled in the same seat they had used that morning. Shelby rested her head against the seat and closed her eyes. "Yeah, I'll figure it out in the morning." She rode back to Wellesley in silence.

CHAPTER 8

Shelby dragged her exhausted body off the bus in front of Peet's. Staring toward Shafer Hall, she sifted through all the information she'd gathered in Boston, trying to fit the pieces together.

"Hey, look who's here." Karl jolted her out of the trance. David had jumped out of his car and was headed in their direction.

"What are you doing here?" Shelby had mixed feelings about his presence.

"I didn't have anything better to do today and … well, I'm really worried about you and your sister." Rumpled clothes and dark rings under his eyes suggested he'd had a sleepless night.

"How long have you been waiting?" Shelby couldn't contain the shock in her voice.

"I'm okay, I just need to know what's happening. Where have you been? Did you find out anything at the police station?" David's urgency flooded her emotions.

Shelby felt exhaustion in every limb. *I can't do this right now,* she thought, her eyes scanning the busy street. They landed on the café they were standing in front of. *He came all this way. He deserves an update.*

"Come on, this is going to require some coffee." She headed toward Peet's with the two guys in tow.

Settling in a quiet corner, Karl made for the counter. By this time he knew Shelby's order by heart and was back at the table with three coffees before Shelby even started explaining the events of the day. She gave David the details of the visit to the police station. He was clearly disappointed that they hadn't made a report. She summarized the stops at all of the hangouts, saving the information they had uncovered on the internet for last.

"So, what are you saying? Do you think that's what happened to Sydney? That she was ..." David was visibly shocked.

"I told her not to jump to outrageous conclusions," Karl chimed in. He still couldn't get his mind around the idea that Sydney might have been kidnapped for exploitation.

"I see what you mean, but terrible things happen because people don't have the guts to look at evil and instead choose to simply ignore the obvious." David spoke with firm conviction.

Shelby was surprised to hear him offer such a philosophical opinion. *Maybe there's more to this guy than I thought.*

"I see what you're saying, but I just can't think of Sydney being used in such a horrible way. She has plans to change the world; she believes people are basically good. I think something like this would break her soul." Karl's voice choked.

Shelby stared at the two guys like she had never seen them before.

"You probably don't know, but Sydney's role model is Gandhi. He survived so many hardships but never lost his faith. Sydney's the same. We'll find her, she's a survivor." Both guys watched her intently.

"What's next?" Karl wanted answers as badly as Shelby.

Before she could answer, their conversation was interrupted.

"I figured you went back to school." Christine appeared, poised and self-assertive at the same time.

The three were stunned into silence. Shelby's heart skipped a beat. *How much should I tell her?*

"We were in Boston," Karl jumped in, "and went to the police station."

Christine didn't show a hint of reaction but responded with what seemed like real concern. "What did you find out?"

Shelby wasn't sure if she should give her the whole scoop but Karl rambled on.

"The police won't file a report until she's missing for forty-eight hours. We talked to some people who did see her but no one had any real answers."

Shelby jumped in, hoping to catch Christine off guard. "One guy told us you were with her."

"Of course, we went to Boston together." Christine seemed defensive.

"Right," Shelby took the offense. "He said you're always there with a different girl. Always only one girl, but a different girl every time. He thought that was kinda odd." She stared into Christine's dark eyes, looking for a reaction.

Christine inhaled deeply and glanced around Peet's. The adjacent table was empty. "Do you mind if I pull up a chair?" She was dragging one over before she'd finished the question.

Karl and David made room; Shelby intently tracked her every move.

"I'm not sure I have to explain myself but since you brought it up … well," she paused and collected her thoughts. "I'm not looking for sympathy, but growing up in a war-torn area makes life difficult. I never had any friends since we had to move around often just to survive. As a result, I'm a bit nervous in groups. So, I like to hang out with only one person at a time. Then I can get to know them and …" tears pooled in her eyes. "I don't know why I'm telling you this. Maybe if you gave me a chance …" She jumped up and bolted from Peet's. Three sets of eyes followed her out the door.

Shelby laid her head on the table and began to sob. The two guys reacted like all guys do when a girl starts to cry. They sat staring at her, clueless.

As her sobs diminished, David reached over to stroke her shoulder.

"Look, Shelby, maybe you need to get some rest, then we can regroup and decide what to do next."

Shelby didn't have energy left to argue. She looked from David to Karl and back again, seeing true concern in their eyes. She dabbed at her tears with a worn napkin.

"You're probably right. So much has happened and I haven't taken a moment to get myself together. I appreciate your support." She grabbed both of their hands, and they flushed in unison.

"When I have a lot on my mind, I make a list," Karl suggested. "Once I have it written down, my mind can rest. After I've slept I'm ready to tackle the challenges."

Shelby opened the notes on her phone and started typing:

> *Call my parents*
>
> *Visit Lt. Down*
>
> *Check around school and find out who the missing girls hung out with*
>
> *Get to know Christine*

David and Karl watched over her shoulder as she typed.

"Do you really want to waste your time with Christine?" David asked.

"She was the last person to see Sydney." Shelby's tone was dismal.

"What are you going to tell your parents?" Karl's worries had deepened.

"The truth." Her answer was short and matter-of-fact.

"When are you going to see Lt. Down?" They quizzed her like she was on trial.

"Okay, okay, look, Karl, you said I need to rest. I agree. How about we meet here in the morning and figure this all out then?" Exhaustion wracked her bones.

"Where are you going to stay?" David had one last question.

"I still have Sydney's key." She pulled it from her pocket and jangled it in their faces.

"You're really going to go stay with her after that little display?" David was clearly not feeling friendly toward Christine.

"She said I should give her a chance, so ..." She stopped short. A plan was formulating, but she wasn't quite ready to share it.

They waited for her to finish, but instead she hauled her weary body from the chair, grabbed her coffee, and headed toward the door.

"What time?" Karl yelled.

"Eight!" The door slammed behind her.

#######################

Christine dialed her mom before she hit the coffee shop exit.

"They went to the police," she blurted.

"Hold on, hold on. What are you talking about? Who? Settle down, give me the story." Christine's mom was a survivor and knew how to diffuse any situation.

"Sydney's twin went to the police in Boston; she's asking around about her sister. She got weird answers about me." Christine was hyperventilating.

"Christine, snap out of it." Her mom's sharp retort stopped Christine short. "Slow down and tell me what they found out. Did the police make a report?"

"No, but ..."

"Why are you getting so worked up over this girl?" She was clearly irritated with her daughter's drama.

"I don't know, there's just something about this situation that's ..." She paused, struggling to make sense of her suspicions.

"Look, just do your job. Your dad and I have made many sacrifices. You owe it to our group to keep your head together." It was a cold response.

Christine's soul caved as her universe crumbled. She hated when her mom used this kind of control. She had no choice but to get her act together.

"Sure ..." came a timid reply. "I just think something is different this time."

"It's not your job to think; your job is to deliver." Her mom's harsh tone ended the conversation.

"I understand. I'll let you know if anything changes." She didn't wait for a response. Hanging up, she crammed the phone into her pocket as she headed to Shafer Hall. *Maybe Shelby will show up and I can work on her some more. When did this get so complicated?* She wrapped her arms around her shoulders as a shiver wracked her body.

CHAPTER 9

Shelby woke to an unexplainable agitation that shook her very soul. Staring into darkness, the only emotion that described the feeling was fear. As the cloud of sleep lifted like a fog burning off a dismal morning, she realized the panic was coming from Sydney. Grasping at the connection, she could see vague shapes in the same room she had perceived before. However, this time Sydney was not alone and an overwhelming fright was coursing through every nerve of her body. Shelby had never known her sister to fear anything. Sydney confronted every challenge in life with a courage that Shelby wished she possessed.

Slowly, it dawned on Shelby that if she focused she could possibly get information regarding her sister's whereabouts. She strained to strengthen the connection and discern any details related to the mysterious surroundings. Sydney wasn't responding. Shelby only felt her sister's suffocating terror.

Then, as quickly as the feeling had started, it vanished. Shelby rolled over and whimpered into her pillow. "No, no, no … we have to stay connected." Struggle as she might, there wasn't even a flicker of her sister's wavelength.

Staring across the room at the shape huddled beneath the comforter, Shelby wondered what Christine wasn't saying. *Despite David's concern, I need to get to know this girl. She was the last one to see Sydney!*

Resolving to follow the plan she'd formulated, she pulled the quilt over her head and wished for sleep. *Sydney, I've got to find you. Give me something to go on. How can I help you?* The thoughts tumbled through her head as she drifted into a fitful slumber.

#######################

As morning crept into the room, Shelby jolted awake and grabbed her phone. It was almost 8 and the guys would worry. The neighboring bed was neat as a pin. Jotting a quick note, she left it on Christine's laptop. Step one of her plan. *I hope she sees that before lunch,* she thought as she dashed out of the dorm.

Stepping into Peet's she saw Karl and David, their heads together in an intense conversation. *I wonder what they're cooking up.* She made her way across the café, phone in hand, requesting an Uber.

"Let's go." Shelby's interruption brought a rapid halt to their discussion. She didn't wait for a response; she simply turned and headed toward the door. When they stopped at the curb, the guys didn't even bother to ask. David handed her a coffee and they waited patiently. Within five minutes a misty blue Camry with an Uber sticker in the window pulled up. A cheerful student jumped out.

"Shelby?" Her dark eyes twinkled despite the early morning hour. It was impossible to miss the dumb look on Karl and David's face. *Guys are all the same when they see a pretty face.*

"Get in!" Her directions got them moving. David popped out of his starry-eyed trance and opened the door for Shelby.

"Where're we headed?" Karl wanted in on Shelby's plan.

"We're headed to see Lt. Down."

"But it's Sunday morning. She won't be there," David said in disbelief.

"I'm ahead of you on that," Shelby half answered as she flipped through the list she had made on her phone the night before. Her fingers were flying across the keyboard as she outlined the plan she had devised in the wee hours of the morning. David shrugged. Karl watched the trees fly by as the Uber navigated the quiet morning streets.

Pulling into the lot of the state police forensic and technology center there was a single car parked in front of the building. Jumping out of the back seat, Shelby noticed a small, trim lady standing at the door, keys in hand.

"Come on, that's her." Shelby took off across the lot.

"Who?" yelled David, chasing after her.

"Lt. Down," she blurted out, not answering David but trying to get the lieutenant's attention.

The lady stopped fussing with her keys and turned to face the three students bearing down on her. "Shelby?"

Karl and David were dumbfounded. Did this lady know Shelby? Shelby inhaled deeply, hoping to summon the courage she'd need to enlist the lieutenant's cooperation.

"Yes, ma'am. I'm very happy that you would take time out of your busy weekend to visit with me … I mean us." Turning to the two guys who were standing with their mouths wide open, Shelby made quick introductions.

"Nice to meet you all. It was no problem to come out. When you said you had information on the missing girls, I had to meet with you immediately. I won't rest until I find them." Lt. Down fidgeted with her keys until she found the right one and pulled the door open, allowing the three to step in ahead of her. Shelby noticed the look that passed between David and Karl. She knew exactly what they were thinking: how had she orchestrated this meeting?

Following the lieutenant down a deserted hall, Shelby studied the rows of vacant cubicles. They were a sharp contrast to yesterday's hectic police station.

"Please come into my office. Have a seat while I make some coffee." She bustled about while they squeezed together on the couch across from her desk.

"What did you tell her?" whispered Karl. "Do you know something new?"

"Shhh …" Shelby gave him the eye, meaning "shut up."

Lt. Down finally settled into her chair with a steaming cup of coffee. She straightened the papers strewn across her desk and then looked hard at Shelby.

"Okay, you got me here. What do you know?"

Shelby's heart was pounding against her chest. She tried to speak but her mouth was so dry she couldn't get her tongue around a single word.

"We're all very concerned about the scene at the local colleges," David said. "It's very scary for girls to be out on their own right now."

"It's a very concerning situation. Human trafficking and the sex trade have grown exponentially. There's more slavery today in the US than during the Civil War when our country fought a bitter battle to put a stop to people owning other humans. It's a situation I'm very passionate about." The lieutenant was getting worked up as she spoke.

While listening, Shelby regained her composure. "I'm here about my sister."

"Oh, one of the missing girls is your sister?" There was doubt in her tone. "We've researched all of their backgrounds and spoken with all of the family members." She stopped and drilled Shelby with her dark eyes. "What's going on?"

"My sister is missing," Shelby gulped. "I need your help ... please," she begged.

"Wait a minute. Who is your sister?"

"Sydney Wilson. She's been missing since Thursday night. I just know something horrible has happened to her, but the police wouldn't help me. I just know she has been taken. I'm so worried." Tears were flowing as Shelby stammered through her concerns.

"Okay, okay, slow down." Lt. Down offered a tissue box and David jumped to retrieve it. "I'm not sure what is going on here. It seems like I'm here on false pretenses. I don't know if I should be angry or …" She stopped short and pulled out a pen and pad. She jotted Sydney's name on the pad and looked at the two guys huddled on each side of Shelby.

"What do you two have to do with this?" There was hostility in her voice and they cringed.

David was the first to speak up. "We're trying to help Shelby find her sister. We really had no idea we were coming here." David flushed, hoping she wasn't going to throw them all out.

Tapping her pen, the lieutenant looked them over very slowly, then asked, "What does Sydney look like?"

Shelby's hands stopped shaking when she realized she was rubbing her tattoo. "Like me exactly. We're identical twins. And she has one of these." She offered her tatted wrist. "Most people can't tell us apart."

"That's true," volunteered Karl. "I've known them both since grade school and still get them confused."

"Okay, I'll take a picture of you before we leave. Tell me why you're so sure that she's in danger and has been taken." She stopped jotting notes and looked straight at Shelby.

"Well ... it's just this thing ... it's just she's my twin ... I know her." She was fumbling for an answer without telling the whole story. "I just know."

"We need a little more to go on than that."

"Tell her," Karl whispered. Shelby gave him the "shut-up eye" again. That was not a road she was prepared to go down yet.

"Tell me what you know." Lt. Down was clearly frustrated, but her years of experience had taught her to follow any lead that might fall in her lap.

Karl finally spoke up. He updated her on what they knew about Sydney's last whereabouts and their visit to the police station. The lieutenant scribbled rapidly on her notepad. When he finished there was an awkward silence. Still huddled on the couch, the trio waited for any response that might give them hope.

Lt. Down stood and ambled around to the front of her desk. Glaring down at the three of them, she shook her head in disbelief. "This was some stunt. There should be some repercussions for getting me out of my house on a Sunday morning. I didn't even finish reading my paper."

They inhaled simultaneously, waiting for her verdict. "Sorry, guys," Shelby murmured.

"But I clearly see you are distraught and it seems something has happened to your sister. I understand that. I'm not sure why you jumped to the conclusions you have, but my gut tells me to listen to your instinct. I can't yet open an official investigation on your twin, but I have your information and will keep my eyes open for anything suspicious. If you can provide me with more specific information, we can proceed." She headed toward the door and the three of them took it as a sign to get moving before she lowered the boom.

"Thank you for hearing us out." Shelby realized she'd taken a big chance and needed to get in the good graces of Lt. Down if she was going to help her find Sydney.

"You obviously have my contact information. So if you have any other information you think would be helpful, feel free to call." After snapping a picture of Shelby on her phone, she let them out the door. Strain drained from their shoulders when they heard the lock behind them.

"Shelby ..." Karl started.

"Sorry, guys, I needed your moral support and I knew you wouldn't go along if I told you where we were going."

"I'd have come," voiced David. For a moment, she wanted to give him a big kiss. *Where did that come from?*

"Let's get an Uber and head back to school," Shelby's racing heart was returning to normal. She realized she didn't have much time to put the next step of her plan into action.

"Now what?" Karl looked at her with doubt written all over his face.

"I'm having lunch with Christine!"

"What?" they blurted out together.

"Yeah, it's time I get to know her. Let's go, there's our ride."

CHAPTER 10

Luan slipped into the dingy office where Vladimir was slumped over his desk making notes in a tattered ledger. He waited patiently until Vladimir lifted his head. There was no need to ruffle feathers before he gave him the news, Luan was sure Vladimir was about to go ballistic.

Vladimir threw his pencil aside and closed the ledger. He inhaled deeply. "So, don't just stand there. What do you know? Have you found him? I want my money back!"

"Well ... I've found him. He's in the US." Luan paused, waiting for the verbal explosion.

"Where?" Vladimir was deep in thought.

"Boston." Luan, proud of his detective work, wasn't sure Vladimir would see it the same way. "Don't you want to know how I found him?"

"I don't care how you found him, I just care that you did." Vladimir's sharp words stung.

Vladimir rose and paced the room, minutes passing. Luan watched him pacing like a caged lion, counting the seconds. Vladimir was a ticking time bomb.

"When will you leave for Boston?" Vladimir looked him square in the eyes, expecting an answer.

Luan, caught off guard, stammered, "What … Well … I mean … I don't have a passport." He cringed, knowing Vladimir hated excuses.

"We have people who can handle that. Get one, get a ticket. I expect you to be on a plane in less than twenty-four hours." He yanked open the drawer to his desk, pulling out a bundle of cash. "Here, don't come back without him." He thought for a moment and chuckled. "If Jetmir doesn't see it my way then bring me that pretty daughter of his. I'm sure that will change his mind."

Luan snatched up the cash and turned on his heel. He'd dodged a bullet. *If things don't work out, maybe I'll just stay in the US with Jetmir,* he thought.

"Hey, Luan, don't cross me," Vladimir warned sternly, as if he'd just read Luan's mind. "Now get out!"

Luan didn't need to be told twice. Stuffing the cash into his jeans, he banged the door closed behind him.

####################

Shelby left the guys standing outside Peet's, promising them an update after her lunch date. She relished the brief stroll to her destination. The sun had moved high in the sky and the warmth loosened her shoulders, draining the stress that had her tied in knots.

Stepping into Bates, Shelby did a once-over of the Sunday brunch crowd. Not seeing who she was looking for, she took a moment and inhaled. *Smells amazing,* she thought. *At least I should grab some food.* Making her way to the omelet station, she dished up an assortment of veggies to complement the eggs. Watching the omelet sizzle, she took a quick mental inventory of her plan. *After lunch, I need to call Mom and Dad. I really can't keep this from them any longer.* Sliding the steaming omelet from the pan to a plate, she scanned for an empty table and saw Christine in the doorway. Their eyes met. Shelby nodded toward a table in the corner. They both headed that direction.

Settling into a small booth, Shelby noticed that Christine didn't have any food.

"Aren't you planning to eat? The omelets look scrumptious." Shelby cringed at herself. She sounded just like that nosy blonde from Peet's.

"I'll get something in a bit. I had a late breakfast." Christine paused, the brief moment of silence hanging like a thick cloud. "I wasn't sure you'd be here." Her eyes searched the dining room, darting from table to table as if she was looking for someone in particular.

"Expecting someone?" Shelby asked, wondering if she was about to be tag teamed.

"Oh no, no …" Christine hesitated. "You wanted to meet?"

"I just thought about what you said last night, you know, that I should get to know you, give you a chance. Sydney's judgment about people rarely fails." Shelby watched Christine as she spoke, not completely sold on Sydney's opinion this time.

"Please eat. Your food will get cold." Christine's voice was soft and reserved.

Shelby picked up her fork and dug in. After a few bites she decided it was time to get the conversation rolling. "So, tell me about life in Kosovo. You know, what's school like, what's day-to-day life like?"

Christine's description of Kosovo was surreal to Shelby. "Well … school isn't like this at all," she gestured around the room. "The educational system is very poor. It's one of the reasons my parents wanted to come here, to give me a better opportunity. Even if I finished higher education there, the job opportunities are nonexistent. About fifty percent of the younger population is unemployed because the economy is so weak. There is a lot of corruption. People just don't trust one another. That makes you feel very alone." She stared off into an invisible world. "I just realized, I think that's why I have such a hard time getting in with a group of girls. I've never really learned to trust."

Shelby felt a tug on her heartstrings. She lived in the US and only truly trusted one person ... her twin. She wasn't sure it made a difference where you lived. Deciding to confide in someone took a lot of courage.

Christine, still caught in her memories, was fiddling with her phone. "Oh, and this," she held up the iPhone, "no one can afford this, or the snazzy computer you left that note on. No one has the money for such nice things."

Shelby had finished her omelet and pushed the plate toward the table edge. One thing was nagging at her. "How did you manage to get here to the US? I know it's hard to get a green card here, especially from certain countries."

"Tell me about it," Christine continued, "We won the immigration lottery."

"What are the odds of that?" Shelby was surprised.

"Something like twelve thousand people applied the year my dad did and the chance to win was like less than .1 percent. We were lucky!" The statistics rolled off her tongue like they were memorized.

"That's pretty amazing. You must feel fortunate to have the opportunity. I guess I kinda take it for granted, even though our parents routinely reminded us to be grateful as we grew up." Shelby suddenly missed her sister more than ever. Sydney was the one individual she relied on. Her sister was the one who knew how to cheer her up when she felt down. *I really need you now, Sydney,* she thought, *you've always been there to solve my problems.* Shelby felt a wave of grief overcome her and tears filled her dark eyes.

"I didn't mean to upset you," Christine sounded sincere, "that's just the way life was there."

"Sorry, it's not your story, it's just …" She needed a quick excuse. "I'm tired and need to get in touch with my parents. I don't know what I'm gonna tell them yet." Playing out her plan was proving harder than she'd anticipated. "Look, maybe we can talk more tonight, if you don't mind me staying one more night in Sydney's space."

"I thought you'd head back to school. You must have classes tomorrow." Christine rose and waited for Shelby to do the same. "But it's okay, I'd enjoy the company."

Either you are who you say you are or you're very convincing, thought Shelby. She didn't know what to think. Grabbing the soiled plate, she made for a bin, depositing it among the other remnants of Sunday's brunch.

"Yeah, I'll probably stay one more night, if you don't mind." Shelby needed time to further her plan.

"Okay then." Christine wore a half smile. "I'm headed to the gym. Catch up with you later."

Shelby watched her intently. She had an itch … something about their conversation wasn't right. Shaking her head like she was trying to knock the pieces loose, she pulled out her phone. *Need to talk to Mom and Dad first.* Finding a bench outside of Bates, she selected "Mom" from her contacts. The third ring got a response. "Mom?"

"Hey, Shelby, are you enjoying your visit with Syd?"

"Yeah, about that," she jumped right in. "I need to tell you something important."

The conversation went much as she'd expected. Mom wanted to know what had happened to her connection with her sister; she was always a believer. Dad, who'd always expressed his doubts regarding his daughters' abilities, felt that Shelby was overreacting. He gave her the same answer as the police officer: she'd turn up! Mom made her promise to let her know as soon as she heard from Sydney.

Karl was her next call. They agreed to meet by the lake in fifteen minutes. Shelby still had that itch and wanted to fill the guys in on the conversation with Christine. She found Karl and David sitting under an aged conifer watching a flock of geese paddling quietly across the still water.

"Hey, guys." They started as if she had snuck up on them.

"What happened?" they blurted out together. It only took minutes for her to update them on the conversation.

It was David who scratched the itch. "Hey, didn't Christine tell us that she was a refugee?"

"That's it! I knew there was something about her story that didn't fit." Shelby felt relief and angst at the same time.

"What's our next move?" Karl needed answers as badly as Shelby.

"Let's find out more about the missing girls. Maybe there's a link Lt. Down hasn't put together. I think I have a piece of the puzzle that she doesn't even know exists." Shelby wanted to confirm her suspicions before she let the guys in on what she was about to do. "Come on, let's find some answers."

They canvased the campus, looking for people who might have known any of the missing students. After several hours they were exhausted and hungry, but they were another step closer to finding Sydney.

CHAPTER 11

Shelby was gone when Christine woke, but she wasn't concerned. The evening chat session had gone as she'd hoped. She dialed her mom, who answered on the first ring.

"What news do you have?" The harsh tone from yesterday's conversation was gone.

"We're on for tonight." Christine was relieved to tell her mom that she'd made progress on their plan. She'd sat up well into the late hours of the night chatting with Shelby, who'd agreed to meet her at the White Horse at 8.

"Same setup." Christine knew the drill. "See you then." Her mom's phone went dead.

Christine set off for Stone-Davis Hall with pancakes in mind.

###########################

Shelby sat outside Lt. Down's office, watching the quiet hum of forensic investigation. It was a stark contrast to the police station she'd visited with Karl. Lt. Down had acknowledged her presence with a brief nod, but was engaged in what appeared to be a heated debate with her junior. Shelby waited patiently.

She mentally reviewed her plans like she was assessing the next move on a chessboard. Last night she'd walked Christine right into the invitation she wanted. She had a few stops to make today, needed to update the guys, and then had to be at the White Horse by 8.

Maybe with a little luck, this will be over by tomorrow. I'm coming, Sydney ... hold on. She hoped Sydney knew she hadn't given up the search.

Lost in her thoughts, she hadn't noticed Lt. Down's presence. The lieutenant broke her concentration. "You're back!"

Shelby, leaping to her feet, fumbled her belongings. She stooped to pick them up from where they'd landed at the officer's feet. Taking a deep breath, she hoped to summon the needed courage. Her eyes met the soft gaze studying her.

"There's more I need to tell you about me and my sister."

"Well come in. Let's hear the rest of the story." Lt. Down directed her to the comfort of the couch. "Would you like some coffee?"

"Thank you, that would be great." Coffee to the rescue. Buzzing for two cups to be brought in, Lt. Down settled next to Shelby, resting her hand on Shelby's knee.

"I was hoping you would come back. That was some stunt you pulled yesterday. Took some guts. I must admit I was a bit irked, but thinking it over I figured there was something you weren't saying."

"Yeah." Shelby's throat was so dry the word barely squeaked out. She sounded like a hoarse frog. *Where's the coffee?*

"You missing your sidekicks?" The lieutenant chuckled at her own wisecrack. The coffee arrived and she handed Shelby the paper cup of courage.

Sipping slowly, Shelby gathered her thoughts and her nerve. "They have no idea I'm here. I needed to tell you some things." She paused. This wasn't a topic she shared … ever!

An expert in reading people, Lt. Down offered gentle encouragement. "All right. I'm here just to listen."

Shelby feared judgment, but saw only compassion on the lieutenant's face. *I wonder how many girls have relinquished their tragic stories to those kind eyes?* Then she realized that their stories were more horrific than she could imagine. That was probably Sydney's story now. That fact alone gave her the fortitude she needed.

Gently rubbing her tattoo, Shelby began, "My sister and I have a special connection, being twins and all. It's been there since I can remember." Pausing, she noticed the lieutenant eyeing the yin-yang tattoo. "This is a permanent reminder of our connection. We can communicate without talking …" she paused, trying to clarify her thoughts.

"How does it work?"

Inhaling deeply, Shelby made up her mind to tell the whole story. "About three years ago, Sydney was out with some friends after a football game. I never went, it just wasn't my thing," Those were the best words to explain her reclusive nature. "It was dark, they were headed to a party. Nat, the driver, was going too fast around a sharp bend. Anyway, it was a horrible accident. Everybody was knocked unconscious. Somehow Sydney barely managed to stay alert. I knew the instant it happened, you know, because of our connection. Using our link, she directed me to where they were. I called for an ambulance and … well, several of the kids were seriously injured. It saved their lives."

"That's quite amazing." There was genuine sincerity in Lt. Down's voice.

"But it didn't turn out so well for me. The cops wanted to know all about how I found them. They treated me like I was somehow responsible for the accident. It's not something Sydney and I had shared with anyone, ever, except our parents. Even our father thinks our connection is a gimmick."

For a brief moment she mentally replayed numerous conversations of their father telling them to "stop the child's play and grow up." Shaking off the memory of his doubts, she continued, "Anyway, the story got around school, and I felt like a freak the way everyone acted."

The lieutenant rapidly put the pieces together. "So tell me what's happened to your sister?"

Relief washed over Shelby, thankful there'd be no ridicule. "Thursday night when I lost our connection, I knew something awful had happened." Tears filled her eyes, but she continued, "I've gotten a couple of brief links. She's in trouble, I just know it. It feels like she's drugged."

Slipping into full detective mode, the lieutenant launched an inquiry. "Do you have any idea where she is?"

"No, not really. She's tied up in some concrete room, very dazed … it's all very foggy."

"Is she injured?"

"I don't think so, but she's afraid. Sydney's never afraid. That really concerns me."

"Is there anyone else around?" The lieutenant was on the hunt.

"There was one time. That's when I really sensed her fear." Shelby stopped and studied the lady in front of her. "You believe me?" It was half question and half a statement of surprise.

"Why wouldn't I? This isn't the first time I've met someone with your particular skill."

Shelby was shocked. Never had she imagined that anyone else could understand the way she and Sydney were connected.

"I'll file a formal report today. We'll need as much information as you can give us." Heading for her desk, the lieutenant's hand hovered over the intercom.

"Wait … there's more." The lieutenant listened intently as Shelby outlined her suspicions regarding Christine.

When Shelby finished, the lieutenant sized her up. "You're very bright. But we need actual proof, not assumptions."

Shelby stood and headed toward the door. "I'll get you your proof!"

######################

Pulling out her phone as she exited the building, she saw that David and Karl had been blowing it up. She shot them a quick text: *meet me at Peet's*. Then she ordered an Uber.

They were all ears as she filled them in on her meeting with the lieutenant. They were in disbelief when she outlined her plan to meet Christine at the White Horse. Despite their adamant protest, in the end they realized they had no say in the decision. Reluctantly, they agreed to their part and promised to go straight to Lt. Down if things went the way Shelby predicted.

CHAPTER 12

Jetmir was sitting at his dented metal desk in the small office beside the holding cell. His ears were deaf to the varied moans and thrashing outside the closed door.

"Yeah," he barked, picking up his phone. His entire body seized up when he recognized the voice.

"How'd you find me?" he asked, trying not to betray his anxiety.

"Wasn't easy," Luan replied, "but you know how insistent Vladimir can be."

"Po," he slipped into his native tongue, "that's why I was done with him." There was dead silence. It fueled Jetmir's distress, the room closing in around him. "Luan?"

"Po." Luan chuckled, knowing he'd cornered Jetmir.

"What's he want?" Jetmir got right to the point.

"His money."

"I don't have his money. What I have, I made here … in the US." Jetmir held his ground.

"That's not how Vladimir figures it. You see, the business is not doing so well without your … what would I call it …" He hesitated. "I'd say your expertise. So, he figures you've taken money from him, money he didn't get a chance to make. Do you see his point?" Luan spoke as if he had the upper hand.

Jetmir got ahold of himself. He'd never thought much of this punk. He was getting irritated. "Can't help it he doesn't have a business mind and he throws his money away on shit," he added, referring to Vladimir's drug habit.

"Not my business. I'm supposed to deliver you with the money." Luan let that hang for a brief moment before hitting him with the next punch. "Or your daughter."

"Screw you!" Jetmir launched his phone across the room where it exploded into pieces against the concrete wall.

Plopping his feet on the desk, he stretched back in his chair. He tried to calm his racing pulse. Staring into nowhere, his mind went to work. He needed to be a step ahead of Luan. The girls in the other room were the least of his concerns right now.

####################

Shelby spent the afternoon organizing the final pieces to put her plan in action. Stepping into the White Horse at exactly 8, she was bewildered. It was a different universe from her last visit, wall-to-wall with students. She saw Steve behind the bar, surrounded rows-deep by loud undergrads. The clink-clinking of the pool balls was masked by feet stomping on the dance floor. She couldn't hear herself think over the earsplitting racket as she scanned the saloon, searching for Christine.

Shoving through the throng of bodies, she finally caught sight of her target hunkered down in a booth near the back of the room. Patting her hip pocket to confirm the tracker was in place, she headed across the room. If this encounter went as planned, she would soon have her sister back.

"Hey," she greeted Christine, and slid into the seat across from her. Christine was silent and seemed caught up in her private world.

Shelby, studying her, couldn't believe that Christine really enjoyed this scene. Hoping to break the ice, she tapped Christine's arm. "Do you get into this?"

Christine jolted as if she hadn't been aware of Shelby. "Oh, no, I was talking to someone," she explained, tapping her earbud.

Seemed more like you were listening, thought Shelby, "Okay. Uh, did you want to get something? You know, to eat or drink."

"Sure." Christine came back to the current moment. "That would be great. What would you like? My treat."

They ordered sandwiches and then silently watched the mob bump and gyrate off one another. When the food arrived, they slipped into a comfortable conversation, picking up where they had left off last night. *I could almost like this girl,* thought Shelby as she weighed the right time to make her move.

The answer presented itself when the blonde from Peet's showed up, "Hi, you two," she started. "It's good to see you again, Sydney," she added in a sugary-sweet tone. Shelby rolled her eyes and didn't answer.

"Let's get out of here." Christine stood up and pushed past the blonde. Heading to pay her tab, Shelby noticed Christine tap the earbud. *Wonder who's on the line.*

Shelby followed close behind. She was sure her heart was going to leap out of her chest. They entered the crowded street, full of students making their rounds of the college hangouts. It wasn't long before a dark sedan pulled up and a window rolled down. "Hey, Christine, you ladies want a ride?"

Here we go, thought Shelby.

"Sure, this is my friend Shelby." Christine made a brief introduction as she climbed into the front seat. Shelby slid into the back and then realized she wasn't alone as she stared into the dark eyes of a hulk-like figure. The locks clicked. Shelby's heart raced. "Mr. Hulk" reached across the seat. She felt a sharp prick followed by a warm rush through her body. The lights went out.

CHAPTER 13

Christine glanced over the seat and saw Shelby slump against the back door.

The driver reached over and patted her shoulder. "You did good, as usual. Your dad will be anxious to work her into the rotation with her twin." A suggestive chuckle came from deep in his throat. Christine felt a shiver shoot up her spine.

The car wound its way through the narrow streets, heading toward the docks. Christine replayed her conversation with Shelby from the night before. It had been pleasant having someone to be "normal" with. But had she, or was it all an act? *There is no normal in my life, she thought, only deception.*

It wasn't long before they pulled up to two large garage doors. Pushing the remote over the visor, the doors parted and the sedan pulled into an old warehouse. The hulk-like guys hauled Shelby's wilted body from the back seat and dumped her on the grungy concrete. She was a limp rag doll. Even with her hair covering her face, Christine knew Shelby was out cold. She hadn't stirred when she'd landed in a heap. Hulk One grabbed the girl under the arms and dragged her toward a cot.

The dark room was vacant except for the row of metal cots lining the far wall. There were moans and groans coming from the sedated figures. Christine blocked the sights and sounds from her mind.

Heading straight for her father's office, she hustled into the room. "Dad, I brought the twin." She couldn't hold back her desire to please her father. Her glee was cut short by the expression on his face.

"What do you mean? I told your mom the pickup was off," he grumbled.

"I didn't know." Christine could tell her father was distraught. Banging through his desk drawers, she saw he was sorting items. Some landed in a metal trash can, others were stuffed into the duffel bag lying on his desk.

"What's happening?" Christine was confused by the change of events.

"We need to get out of here." Her dad meant business. "We're going … now," he added sternly, throwing a match into the metal can.

"What about my stuff?" She realized she sounded like the child of years ago. Her mind was spinning back to all the times they'd made an unexpected move. It never ended well.

"We'll get your stuff. Come on, let's go." He pushed past her, heading for his SUV.

Christine felt like deadweights anchored her feet.

"What about them?" she pointed toward the holding cell.

"They'll be fine. Now let's go." This time it was an order.

She headed toward her dad's car, tears rolling down her cheeks. *What is this?* she wondered. She didn't dare admit that she felt a wave of remorse.

CHAPTER 14

David stared at Karl's computer as he worked the tracking program they'd installed that afternoon.

"You sure that thing really works?" The strain in his voice stopped Karl from fidgeting with the program.

"We better hope so!" Karl's nerves were overloaded.

"It's going to be a long night." David lay back on Karl's bed and said a silent prayer.

######################

David slowly stirred, then bolted upright. He had no idea how long he had been asleep. Shaking out the creaks and cramps, he saw Karl hunched over his computer and staring at the screen like it was a magic crystal ball.

"What time is it?" David rubbed his eyes and peered over Karl's shoulder. "What do you know?"

"First question, it's 7 a.m." Karl was completely engrossed in the screen.

"Have you been at this all night?" David watched in disbelief.

"Well, yeah, I've been monitoring to see if she was moved. They have her at this warehouse by the docks." He pointed to a Google map of the port area. "She's been there since she left the White Horse." Karl stretched. "I put the location in my phone. I think we can find it."

"You're not thinking of going there to save her, are you?" There was mild panic in David's voice.

"No way. We're doing exactly what Shelby said. We're going to see Lt. Down." Karl grabbed his jacket and headed for the door.

"That sounds just as freaky as taking on the bad guys." David followed him out the door, hoping Shelby's plan was solid.

######################

Shelby stirred, trying to clear the fog from her mind. Rolling over, she realized she was chained to a metal bed frame. Fear reached out and clutched her heart in its clammy hand. She stared into the dark, trying to orient herself. Then she heard the inner voice that had vanished days ago.

"Shelby, I need your help." There it was, right where it had been all her life. Her connection with Sydney was restored. That was all she needed to pull herself together.

"Sydney, I'm here. Where are you?" Blinking rapidly, she tried to make out her sister's shape in the dark warehouse.

"I'm so relieved to have you back. It's been horrible."

Shelby experienced a full range of emotion coming from Sydney's response.

"Sydney, I'm here!" Shelby attempted to calm her sister's panic.

"I know, I just need to figure out where I am so you can come for us, like you did before. These girls need…. we all need your help."

Shelby realized her sister still didn't understand the communication.

"Sydney, I'm trying to tell you, I'm here. Where you are. I was brought here last night." Shelby felt a shock wave pulse through her sister.

"What do you mean! Why?"

"Sydney, it's okay, it's all going to be okay."

"You have no idea what's going on. It's not okay." Sydney's panic flooded Shelby's very soul.

"Listen, Sydney, they're coming for us, we're going to be fine." For the first time in their life it was Shelby who had the situation under control.

"What's going on?" Sydney's confusion continued to seep through Shelby.

"I let Christine pull me into her web. I figured out her little game."

"Christine....we can talk about her later. For now, how are we getting out of here?"

Shelby started to chuckle. "Our valiant knights are coming."

"Come again?"

Shelby knew, Sydney wasn't feeling the promise of a rescue.

CHAPTER 15

Lt. Down looked like she was about to blow the roof off the building.

"What kind of crazy idea was this? You have no idea what you're getting into. These are dangerous people who do horrible things and she just waltzed into their lair like she was going to—" She stopped ranting but continued pacing, her mental wheels turning. David and Karl sulked like two kids who'd been reprimanded for stealing cookies.

"Okay." She was slowing down, a locomotive running out of steam. "Give me the location you tracked her to." The lieutenant called in reinforcements. In no time her team was up to speed.

Spreading a map across her desk they quickly devised the tactics to take the warehouse from all sides. Rescuing the girls was the first objective, but they didn't want anyone responsible for this network to slip out a back door.

Karl and David backed against a wall and watched the flurry of activity. Lt. Down barked a few last orders, then her team headed for the door.

"We're coming with you," Karl blurted.

The lieutenant stopped in her tracks and glared. David met her eyes with equal intensity, it was clear they weren't backing down.

Lt. Down studied the two. "All right, but stay out of the way!"

The Boston police had been contacted. Their SWAT team pulled into the staging area at the same time the lieutenant arrived with her squad. After outlining the plan, the police detective ordered his team to take up strategic locations around the building.

It was early morning, but the port area was beginning to come alive. Crowds were gathering behind the barricades that had been erected. Karl and David were huddled behind a squad car taking in the strategy that the lieutenant had organized.

Lt. Down hoped the criminals would come out peacefully but knew that was a pipe dream. Bullhorn in hand, she barked orders: "We have the building surrounded! Come out with your hands up." The clock ticked; no response.

"How long do they wait?" David nudged Karl. "Will they go in firing?"

"This isn't TV, they need to follow protocol. Now shhh ..."

David struggled to calm his racing heart. He prayed the girls wouldn't be used as hostages.

#######################

"Did you hear that?" Sydney was alert to the sounds inside and out. "Something has changed."

"I told you we'd be rescued." Shelby was relieved that her plan was coming together.

"No, I mean there's no sound in the office." Sydney strained to hear the familiar sounds of Jetmir and his crew. The SUV was gone. No guards posted. Shelby was receiving the ideas as quickly as Sydney sorted it out.

"They're gone!" They reached the conclusion simultaneously. "Heeeelp, heeeelp, heeeelp ..." they screamed. The startled girls in the holding area joined in, shrieking like their lives depended on it.

"Listen!" Outside, Lt. Down was horrified by the commotion. "Let's go!" She was terrified the girls' lives were at risk. Her squad mobilized quickly, guns drawn. The SWAT team battered the door. Fanning out in the dark room, letting their eyes adjust, the shouts stopped abruptly. Then there was silence. What had happened? Were the girls all right?

The lieutenant stood taking in the scene. Gradually, her eyes focused. She could make out the small shapes tied to the row of metal cots. She scanned for any targets, saw the small office, and made a beeline hoping to capture someone. The lieutenant rammed open the door and was overpowered with the stench of an extinguished fire. Otherwise, the room was empty.

"All clear," she shouted.

"Over here!" Shelby yelled.

Within minutes, the girls were surrounded by battle-ready officers. They quickly assessed the scene, laid down their guns, and went to work releasing each girl from her personal prison. The metal cots had been bolted to the concrete and each girl was cuffed by an ankle to a bed frame. Their panic seemed to ebb as they gradually realize that they had been found. Tears flowed.

The police scattered through the building, searching every nook and cranny for the kidnappers. The lieutenant's team moved from girl to girl, checking vitals.

Karl had located Sydney on her cot. Kneeling beside her he gently caressed her shoulder, uttering over and over, "I knew your sister could find you."

Lt. Down didn't waste any time finding Shelby. "This rescue was a harebrained idea! It could have ended very differently."

"But it didn't! I knew I could find her!" Shelby wasn't backing down. For once in her life she wasn't going to stand in the shadows and feel like a freak. She was proud of what she'd accomplished. "Yes, I risked my life for my sister," she paused, "and I'd do it again!"

The lieutenant sensed Shelby's resolve. Her aggression ebbed; her soft side cracked from its shell. "Shelby, you found them! They all owe you a huge debt."

Huddled on the edge of the cot that had been her prison, Shelby gazed around the holding cell. The girls were in various stages of shock and malnutrition. Then it hit her. *I could've been one of them. This has got to stop. No one should ever be used like a piece of property … ever!*

"I understand why you do what you do," she said solemnly to the lieutenant. "Did you catch the guys responsible? Did you find Christine?"

"Something scared them off. Any idea?" Lt. Down needed a resolution. She was relieved to have the girls freed, but the abductors were still out there. She knew they would steal someone's life again. As long as they were at large, her job wasn't done. "Did you see or hear anything that would explain the rapid exit?"

"Truthfully, I didn't hear or see anything after I was drugged. The first thing I recall was having Sydney back. You know …" Shelby swiped at a tear that slipped down her check. "I need to see her now. Where is she? I have to see her with my own two eyes."

"Sure, over here." Lt. Down rose. "We'll talk more later. I need to wrap this scene first." All business again she turned toward the police chief that passed by, then stopped as she watched the two girls reunite. "Shelby, I'm so happy you have your sister back."

The twins stared into each other's eyes. No words were spoken; they exchanged their relief through their private connection. They had all they needed now … each other.

The guys stood silently and watched as Sydney and Shelby held onto one another like long- lost relatives.

Shelby was the first to speak, pulling Karl and David into the reunion. "These two are our knights in shining armor."

Huddled in a four-way hug, tears flowed from all eyes.

CHAPTER 16

The rest of the day was a blur. The girls were checked by doctors. Two were rushed to the hospital. Sydney insisted she stay with her sister. The warehouse was turned upside down, digging for any clue that could explain the quick departure. Lt. Down was all business but kept checking back with Sydney and Shelby as they were hustled between detectives. She was still in disbelief that Shelby had pulled off her scheme.

Following some lunch, they were transported to the state police forensic facility. They answered more questions and worked with artists who drew sketches of faces they could remember. Over and over, they elaborated on the events of the past few days. Shelby provided the information she had gathered around campus. Sydney filled in the bits she could remember, including names and faces of the "gentlemen" callers that had been forced on her. Hotels were contacted, hoping they could provide names, phone numbers, or credit card info. Someone had paid for the rooms. The school must have some information on Christine's parents. No stone was left unturned. Lt. Down's facility was a madhouse of activity.

It was late when the girls returned to the dorm. The room was a shambles. Making their way through clothes and debris thrown around the floor, they tried to figure out where Christine could have gone. Another quick exit, but not before she'd quickly scratched out a few words. They found the note stuck to Shelby's computer. It read: *Shelby and Sydney, I'm sorry!*

"Well, that adds another mystery to the story, doesn't it?" Shelby paused. "You know I spent quite a bit of time talking to her the past few days. I think she's as much a victim as you were. I'm afraid she has no way out of her prison."

"I think you're right. She doesn't have a sister like you to rely on." Sydney wrapped her arms around Shelby. "We're so blessed."

Shelby took a moment to hold onto her sister. Then she picked up her phone.

"We should let Lt. Down know." Explaining the scene they'd walked into, she gave a quick "yep" and hung up.

"She wants to send a team over in the morning to see if they can pull any prints," Shelby explained. "Will that be a problem?"

"I'll get the okay in the morning. For now, I just want to get some food and sleep in my own bed." Sydney's voice was strained. The past few days had taken a toll.

Sydney moved about her room, putting things in order. Digging out some PJs, she slipped into them and crawled into her bed.

"Shelby, how did you come up with the plan?" Her voice cracked.

Shelby climbed into the bed and snuggled next to her. "I just did what you would've done." Then, ever so nonchalantly, she added, "I can't live without you here." She tapped her head and then her heart.

Sydney laid her head on Shelby's shoulder and took a deep breath. "How about a pizza?"

"Yeah, the usual?" Shelby was already dialing. "And when I finish the order, I should call Mom and tell her all is fine, leaving out the details of my plan … okay?"

"Shelby, I think we both need Mom's touch right now. Ask her to come….okay?"

"Yeah," Shelby closed her eyes and listened to her sister's heartbeat. It was the best thing she had heard in days.

CHAPTER 17

Christine hadn't spoken since they left Boston. They had been on the road for twenty-four hours when she finally broke her silence.

"Where're we headed?" she asked as the black SUV passed through the border patrol into Mexico.

"Cancun. Lots of parties there," her mom answered.

Christine slumped down in her seat. Something had changed for her. She was weary from her job as the setup.

"You know," she mumbled, "I'm not any different than those girls back in the warehouse."

"How do you figure?" her father grumbled.

"I'm being forced to do something I don't agree with and I have no way out." Tears streamed down her face.

"I'm doing this to protect you."

"From what? What could be worse than this?" she shot back.

"It's not your place to question my decisions." She saw her father's stern look in the rearview mirror; the discussion was over. She closed her eyes and slumped deeper in the seat.

####################

The twins met the guys at Peet's the next morning. David gathered the order and headed to a quiet table in the back where the girls were settled with Karl. They sat quietly sipping their coffee and munching croissants. The guys watched the girls intently, wondering when to break the silence. Finally, Sydney dabbed at a few crumbs and sat back, heaving a huge sigh.

"That tasted amazing. The simple things! I wasn't sure I'd ever enjoy those again." All eyes at the table were staring at her. "I'm okay, guys, I didn't break."

"What's next?" Karl spoke with reserve.

"I'm going to get some counseling, I have to meet with a doctor, and the police still have questions ... for both of us," she added, looking at Shelby. "I suppose it will take some time to get over this. But I think it's best if I keep busy. I want to get back to my goals. I'm more intent than ever on finishing my studies in Peace and Justice."

"But …" Karl paused, "how can you … I mean," he stammered. "There won't be any justice."

"How do you know? Gandhi said, 'There is a higher court than courts of justice and that is the court of conscience. It supersedes all other courts.' I'm not going to let this incident ruin my life. I can be a victim or I can be a survivor. I choose the latter." Karl's eyes were full of admiration.

"What about you, Shelby?" David was anxious to hear her plans.

"Well, mom's coming today. After filling her in on the past few days I'm going to get you to take me back to school." She winked. David blushed. "In all seriousness, I've spent some time talking to Lt. Down. I'm going to change my major to criminal justice. I need to make a change in the world too, and I think I have a mind for that line of work."

"You proved that. All those girls owe you their lives. Including me!" Sydney wrapped her arm around her sister's shoulders.

"Hey, it's a double take!" Their favorite blonde interrupted the moment.

Shelby rolled her eyes. Sydney reached out her hand. "Have you met my amazing sister? This is Shelby. You may have read how she saved the girls who were kidnapped."

"No ... Uhhh." There was shock on her face. "Wow ... cool ... gotta go." She turned and bolted. The guys burst out in hearty laughter.

"Hey, someday she'll realize," Sydney quickly defended the blonde as she waltzed away. "It just takes some people longer than others to grow up."

"Syd, I'm going to let you two have a few quiet minutes together." Shelby jumped up. "Come on, David." He followed her toward the door like a puppy.

She turned at the door and looked back at Sydney and Karl huddled together at the table. Sydney looked up. Shelby touched her heart and blew a kiss.

It was returned with a mental "Love you!"

FACTS ON HUMAN TRAFFICKING

Human trafficking is defined as holding or transporting people, often by use of force, fraud, or coercion, for commercial or sexual exploitation. According to some estimates, approximately 80 percent of trafficking involves sexual exploitation and 19 percent involves labor exploitation.

Although slavery is commonly thought to be a thing of the past, human traffickers generate hundreds of billions of dollars in profits by trapping millions of people in horrific situations around the world, including here in the U.S. Traffickers use violence, threats, deception, debt bondage, and other manipulative tactics to force people to engage in commercial sex or to provide labor or services against their will. Victims of trafficking can be any age and gender.

Every continent in the world has individuals who are held in bondage. In the United States, it is most prevalent in Texas, Florida, New York, and California.

Education is the number-one way to prevent human trafficking! I hope this story, although it is fiction, increased your awareness of how easily one can be pulled into such a trap. If you suspect someone is in a compromised situation, please use the following contact information:

National Human Trafficking Hotline (from the National Human Trafficking Resource Center)

- 1-888-373-7888

- Website: https://humantraffickinghotline.org/

- Available 24 hours per day, seven days a week.

Can provide assistance in more than 200 languages.

ABOUT THE AUTHOR

My love of reading began as soon as I learned to decode letters. Reading voraciously, I learned how to write. My love for children guided me into the field of education. My desire to help others brought these two passions together. How can one look around the world and not want to change what they see? I write to communicate to the next generation in a way that they will hopefully strive to make our world a better place.

I'M NOT FOR SALE

www.ingramcontent.com/pod-product-compliance
Lightning Source LLC
Chambersburg PA
CBHW071126250626
47159CB00006B/2149